My Highland Billionaire

Shelley Munro

MUNRO PRESS

My Highland Billionaire

Print ISBN: 978-1-99-106371-7
Ebook ISBN: 978-1-99-106370-0

Editor: Evil Eye Editing
Cover: Kim Killion, The Killion Group, Inc.

Munro Press, New Zealand.

First Munro Press electronic publication December 2024
First Munro Press print publication December 2024

DEDICATION

For Paul, my husband, partner in crime, and fellow
adventurer.
Every day is a good day.

INTRODUCTION

Curiosity landed the cat hip-deep in trouble...

Feline shifter Suzie Paisley and her friend have ambitious plans, but when her longtime sidekick meets a man and disappears without a word, Suzie is distraught. Before she can regroup, her inquisitive nature throws her in the path of a Highlander bear shifter. Mistake. Big mistake because now the sexy bear is holding her captive in a castle tower.

Experience means Niall Sinclair doesn't trust easily, and he's kicking himself after learning his impatience might've placed his new product at risk. Then there's the cute New Zealand shifter currently locked in his tower. His bear half wants her badly, but corporate espionage is a thing. Is he inviting the enemy into his home? No! He'll blackmail her into his way of thinking and send her home once his honey hits the market. No harm. No foul.

My Highland Billionaire contains a grumpy versus sunshine vibe, mistaken identity, revenge, suspense, and scars from the past—a lot to work through before Suzie and Niall reach their happy ever after. Let's hope they have staying power!

1

PLAYING HOOKY

THE CASTLE INTERIOR WAS vast, and Suzie explored each day, poking into rooms filled with elegant furniture and valuable paintings, walls of books, and an enormous snooker table. She loved the feminine bedrooms with their attached dressing rooms and the bathroom she'd discovered with an old clawfoot tub in excellent condition.

Attending the Highland Gathering events took up most of her time. Despite her unwillingness, she'd mingled with other single shifters and participated in activities because Saber Mitchell and London Drummond had asked her to represent Middlemarch.

This morning, her steps dragged, her enthusiasm at an all-time low. Edwina had gone. Her best friend had left with the handsome man who'd carried her from the ballroom. She hadn't boxed his ears or slapped his face. She hadn't marched back into the castle, indignant at his cheek.

She'd vanished.

Suzie sighed and tried not to think ill of her friend.

Each of the six shifters from Middlemarch had known they might find a mate among the gathering attendees, but Suzie had started to relax. She and Edwina would successfully navigate the gathering to take up their university places in Wellington. They'd upskill together as they'd planned.

Suzie slowed as she took in the portraits. The subjects stared disapprovingly and arrogantly from their frames. She sighed again, depression taking a grip.

Dark thoughts.

Why me pity.

Anger at her friend despite the unfairness of her thoughts.

Saber and London had explained how difficult it was to ignore a mate bond, and Suzie had seen evidence of this truth this week. Hormones and nature were a bitch, especially if you had shifter blood.

Muttering under her breath and cursing fate, she strolled through a reception room and past a gleaming suit of armor. A delicate marble urn sat in an alcove, a spotlight showcasing the sheer beauty of the artistry. She wandered through a short passageway and lingered in front of a staircase. A chain hung across the stairs as a flimsy barrier with a sign attached that read *Private. No admittance.*

That sign had taunted her since day one of her arrival at the gathering.

Curiosity nagged at her, diverting her dark mood.

Questions.

She'd grilled Angus Falconer, the castle steward, and he'd told her Castle Glenkirk had been rundown and unkempt until a Scottish billionaire had purchased the property and set about restoring it to its former glory. Not the current owner, though. He'd inherited the property. Angus had told her the man's name: Niall Sinclair. Her internet search had turned up surprisingly little, and Angus steadfastly refused to give her more than the basics.

A thought prickled through her mind, and her breath caught. She glanced left and right and couldn't see any staff or guests. Suzie stepped closer to the sign before the impulse even registered. A second later, she was tiptoeing lightly up the stairs and around the corner.

Her pulse raced, and she fleetingly wondered what trouble might result from her nosiness. *Gah!* The worst they could do was kick her out of the gathering, which would suit her fine. The number of shifters had dwindled, although rumor told her more would show tomorrow. New arrivals brought the risk of her finding a mate, ruining her plans.

When she reached the top, she hesitated over which direction to explore. Her instincts prompted her to the right.

Angus had told her the owner lived in the castle, so it made sense that the rooms on this level mixed antiques with modern living. The deep chocolate brown couches were comfortable and built on the sturdy side. She could imagine a man lounging here, watching a rugby game while drinking a glass of Scottish whisky. Well, almost. Nowhere in this room could she see a large-screen television.

"Where the devil have you been?"

Suzie jumped at the irate Scottish burr and opened her mouth to apologize and explain she'd taken a wrong turn while searching for a bathroom. She faced the grumpy man, and her mouth dried of spit. While she was trying to corral her thoughts, the handsome, suit-wearing lug continued his tirade.

"I expected you an hour ago. Well, come along. Stop dithering. We have work to do."

And he was massive. Freakin' huge, standing at what she'd guess would be around six foot five. His designer suit highlighted his broad shoulders and narrow waist but concealed his musculature. Given the breadth of him, the man would possess decent muscles.

Be still my heart.

His dark brown hair was thick and unruly and fell in messy waves. Then there was his Scottish accent, rough and deep and perfect. She barely resisted the urge to pat her galloping heart.

The behemoth issued a harsh sigh and scowled. "Why are you dallying, woman? Don't the employment agencies check their temp workers for wits? What was Angus thinking? Letting you wander on your own."

Suzie scowled back, even as her mind worked at a furious pace. He'd mistaken her for someone else. That was clear. She started to put him straight before clicking her teeth together and rethinking her strategy. Tired of assessments from shifters with a mate bond in mind, she had reached her *activity* limit. With his Mr. Grump tendencies, this man had pushed her woe-is-me attitude out of her mind.

Before he could strike her with another salvo of rudeness, she said, "What did you require? Sir." She tacked that bit on the end because, given his designer suit and presence in the private part of the castle, he might be important.

"I have documents to type." He paused, giving her a searching glance. "Do you do dictation?"

"Yes." That wasn't a lie. She'd aced her secretarial course and enjoyed learning the different aspects of what made an excellent personal assistant. She could type, copy, computerize, and organize with the best of them.

Given his size, Suzie imagined he'd command respect because his presence filled the room.

"Humph!" His sharp grunt combined arrogance, doubt, and annoyance in equal measures. "Come along then, and we'll see if you speak the truth."

Once again, she yanked at the reins of restraint and pressed her lips together to prevent an indignant retort. She'd rather hide up here than face the fresh shifters with uncrushed enthusiasm or the desperate ones. That group was worse because of their urgency and the driven nature of their actions and conversation.

The big man stalked across the cream and terracotta French Aubusson carpet while Suzie followed more slowly, taking in the rug's central medallion and floral border. She knew from her research since she'd arrived at the castle that the rug was an antique and worth many thousands.

They entered an adjoining room with a massive oak table, but she didn't have time to dally and admire anything else. One more left turn, and they entered a modern office.

The grumpy behemoth pointed at a wooden desk. "That is your station. Coffee machine is there, and if you're hungry, there's food in the fridge." He indicated a wooden cabinet, and she presumed the unit concealed the fridge.

The truth—it was difficult to concentrate on what he was saying because his sexy accent kept distracting her. She'd bet the man could read the driest document and make it seem alluring.

"My desk." He gestured at a massive desk with orderly piles of papers, books, and a computer. "Do not chatter, hum, or tap your fingers on the desktop. Do not play on your phone or answer personal calls during work time. Is that clear?"

"Crystal," Suzie said.

His hazel eyes were so beautiful—way too gorgeous for this grumpy man. They narrowed a fraction more, emitting clear suspicion. He didn't think she was listening.

"Make our coffee, and we'll start on the dictation after you sign the non-disclosure document. I want to record my thoughts while they're fresh."

Suzie barely stopped herself from giving a two-finger salute. A non-disclosure document? Color her even more curious. This man was a grumpy, snarly mountain of flesh, but he'd alleviated her boredom and despair. She took a quick breath because his sudden appearance had left her instinct flagging and her mouth hanging open.

His scent filled her nostrils—tangy with an undertone of sweetness—a syrupy tartness with hints of heather and whisky.

He was a bear.

Of course, he was, now that she added the clues. Large—check. Short-tempered—check. Brown hair—hmm, perhaps a brown bear?

"What are you waiting for? I'm not paying you to stand around gawking."

He wasn't paying her at all. Not that it mattered. She didn't have to take his snapping and snarling. Yes, she'd been trespassing and deserved chastisement for that crime. She opened her mouth to unleash a verbal assault and changed her mind. Her thoughts buzzed with curiosity, and she desperately wanted to learn what required a non-disclosure document from a lowly temp.

Besides, her alternative was to return to the gathering activities and fake a smile for the desperate and the newbies. Now that Edwina had gone, the gathering had lost its luster.

Suzie marched to the coffee machine and selected a pod containing industrial-strength caffeine. For herself, she chose one flavored with vanilla. Soon, the coffee scent perked her up, and she delivered the burly bear his steaming mug. She grabbed a pad of paper and two pens and planted herself in the chair opposite him.

"This is the non-disclosure document. Think carefully before you sign it because not even a top-notch lawyer will get you out of the problems I will heap on you should you decide to sell any proprietary information. Why are you wearing that weird, gawking expression? The employment agency must've told you I expected you to sign this agreement before you commenced work for me."

"I have no problem signing a non-disclosure, but I would like to read the terms and scope of it first," Suzie said, her voice professional and polite.

The starch exited him, and he gave a tiny nod of what might be approval. He handed over a document. Huh, more than the one page she'd expected. Her eyebrows winged upward, and she shot him a glance. His face remained expressionless. Wow, his was a resting grump face if ever she'd seen one.

She turned her attention back to the document and started reading. At the end of page one, she sipped her coffee. *Yum, that was delicious.* After another quick taste, she glanced at the bear. Heck, she didn't even know his name and didn't want to ask because the employment agency would've told her. Wouldn't they?

She kept reading, the clauses long and convoluted but reasonable, given the circumstances. Whatever he was working on was top-secret and commercially vulnerable. A product in development. Her brow creased before she consciously smoothed it. A bad habit, and according to her grandmother, she'd develop early wrinkles. Suzie read to the end and hesitated, her pen hovering over the signature spot. Maybe it was best for her to confess she wasn't the temp he was expecting except...

She battled with her conscience, her boredom, and her love of adventure.

And failed to do the right thing.

Yet again, her grandmother would say.

Suzie signed the document with a flourish and handed it to him. If the temp showed up, she could talk her way out of trouble. She surreptitiously crossed her fingers. *Hopefully*.

After another sip of her excellent coffee, she arched her brows, attention on him as she held her pen poised over the pad. While dictation wasn't her favorite thing, she was no slouch and confident in her ability.

He started slowly as if doubting her skills, but once he saw she didn't falter, he sped up. Leaning back in his chair, his eyes partially closed, he focused on spouting facts about honey production.

Suzie almost laughed at the cliche, and losing focus had her pen spluttering to a halt. "Sorry, could you repeat that?"

Honey? Hardly a groundbreaking secret. Honey was a subject she knew little about, apart from the fact it tasted delicious spread on her favorite granary bread, and her father was rather partial to a teaspoon in his hot toddy.

The man glowered at her, but instead of being intimidated, Suzie saw the growly bear more clearly. He wasn't handsome in the traditional sense—she'd describe him as rugged—but his hazel eyes drew the gaze. They were stunning, surrounded by the long, dark lashes women strove to possess. And again, that sexy accent...

He gave his head a faint shake and plunged back into the dictation, moving on to the marketing aspect. Suzie's pen raced across the page while she listened to his rough Scottish accent and assimilated the information. She found it fascinating. Honey was to him what music was to her, a surprising revelation.

Finally, he stopped speaking and picked up his empty coffee mug. "More."

She stared at him before accepting the mug, but he plowed into returning phone calls.

"No, Michael. That's fine. Harris is working this morning. He'll take care of the honey for me. Your time is better spent at the plant. Aye, I'll let you know if I need you." He hung up and punched in another number.

Suzie shook away the accent-induced trance and ceased her eavesdropping to focus on the coffee. After taking her temp boss's mug over to him and receiving a grunt, she assumed he'd want her to type these notes in readable form.

Suzie sipped her vanilla coffee and quickly found the relevant programs to do her thing. While the notes were comprehensive, they raised questions. She swiftly glanced at her growly boss, who appeared immersed in a sheaf of papers.

She shrugged inwardly and wrote her comments and questions in red italics beneath each point that made her curious. Some bosses liked their secretaries or personal assistants to use their initiative. She wasn't sure which camp he fell into, but she'd learn soon enough.

Suzie completed transcribing her dictation and read through what she'd written. It was correct, and she felt her comments were relevant. She sent the document to a printer and stood to retrieve it. After another quick check, she took them to her temp boss.

"What is so great about this honey?" she asked, hoping she received more than snarls in reply.

"What?" he asked absentmindedly. His hair stood in tufts, although she hadn't noticed him dragging his hand through his curls.

"Why is this honey important to you? Is it a bear thing?"

Niall jerked his attention from his research and formulas to gawk at her. Had he heard right?

"Are you obsessed with this honey because you are a bear?" she asked.

Genuine curiosity sat on her features. She didn't mean to sound rude, or perhaps she did. Her green eyes certainly twinkled with mischief.

"Have you transcribed my notes?" he snapped.

"Yes."

And to his surprise, she handed over the printed version. He scanned them rapidly and did a double take. She dared to pencil in comments. His brows squeezed together, his eyes widening at her concise wording and questions. *Very interesting*.

He lifted his head and honestly looked at her for the first time today. She had long black hair and green eyes that reminded him of the jade he'd seen during a visit to China three years ago. Her skin was fair but held the faint kiss of the sun, which led his thoughts in an entirely unprecedented direction. He wrenched his gaze away, his heart thumping against his rib cage. Despite that, her oval face remained in his mind's eye, her small straight nose and full lips devoid of lip color. She wasn't tall because he towered over her, but he dwarfed most humans. This one wasn't human, though. His nostrils flared, his senses catching more now that he fully engaged them.

Feline.

"Please, can you tell me what is so special about your honey?" That was interest in those fascinating green eyes and an Antipodean accent. His last secretary hadn't cared and had never asked questions, apart from requesting a raise for sub-par work.

"My honey has the usual health benefits. It is rich in nutrients and antioxidants. It has antibacterial properties that can soothe burns and sore throats. But it also has an added component, an unexpected benefit." Pride rose in him because this was a freakin' miracle. "My honey increases performance in speed and strength." He paused for her reaction, and she didn't disappoint him.

"How? Do you mean if I ate your honey, I could raise heavy weights above my head?"

A startled laugh escaped him. "Do you normally lift heavy weights?"

She wrinkled her nose. "That will never happen."

He stared for a beat longer and experienced the strange urge to laugh. Quite unlike him. What magic did the woman use? He was driven. Exacting. He expected his employees to work hard and rewarded them well for their labor. He relied on instinct, along with research and careful plans. His goal: to become successful enough that his family would finally pay attention to him instead of ignoring him as the runt of the litter. It shouldn't, but their lack of support hurt, and he was determined that one day, they would see him as a successful businessman.

Her dark brows knit together in a fierce frown. "How are heavy weights related to your honey?"

He saw no harm in telling her since she'd signed a non-disclosure. "I've discovered if a training athlete eats my honey, they gain the benefits of increased speed, increased strength. My honey is a natural performance-enhancing drug. Taking the honey has no side effects or rule violations."

"Wow! That has far-reaching implications. What if you tested your honey on a person with a physically demanding job? Would it make a difference?"

Hellfire! How had he missed that angle? "So far, I have worked with two athletes who are personal friends. Regular consumption of my honey has made me faster. I've cut several seconds off my best time on my daily runs. My runner friend regularly wins races when he'd be lucky to place before. The other friend specializes in decathlon, and his all-around improvement has thrilled his coaches. I've also approached a gym to use my honey in their drinks and monitor user performance."

"That is all the testing you've done?"

"So far. I'll do further testing before I market my product, but I need to find more trialists," he muttered, more to himself than her.

"Perhaps I could find test subjects for you. How long until the honey works?"

"The effects are almost immediate. After eating a slice of toast and honey or adding a teaspoon to a cup of tea, my friends and I noticed increased energy. But I don't want my honey to go to too many people because if competitors get wind of my creation, they'll try to steal my formula. The honey world is cut-throat, and some of my competitors lack scruples."

The woman laughed. What was her name, anyway? He hadn't thought to ask. Something about her knocked him off-stride. No, perhaps it was best to focus on his goal. He did *not* need a woman interrupting his smooth forward progress.

"Why are you laughing?" he asked belatedly.

"I'm trying to imagine a group of guys in white suits with those special masks they use while collecting honey from the hives, and each of them engaged in fisticuffs."

Niall's mood went from perplexed to angry with one quick blink. "This is not a laughing matter. And there would be no fisticuffs involved. I suggest you search online for honey thefts and read the stories. That will stop your humorous flights of fancy."

She gawked at him, her green eyes wide, and he could tell she didn't believe him.

"I had a security man injured last year. He still can't work because the thieves beat him so badly. All they wanted was honey to sell on the black market. They didn't care who they hurt or what they needed to do to steal my product."

She pressed her lush lips together, and everything inside him went still. His bear loosed a lusty sigh that, thankfully, remained inside his mind and not out in the open for her to hear. He cast his mind back and silently cursed.

Why hadn't he asked her for her name instead of merely ordering her to start work?

"Is honey that valuable then?" she asked.

"It's liquid gold and very profitable if you hit the market right. Consumers are searching for natural products these days. They want to feel good about themselves and purchase the best they can afford."

"A status thing," she scoffed.

"Don't knock it. Honey is paying your wages."

A strange expression bolted over her face, lightning-fast and way too speedy for him to decipher.

"Should I try to work out a list of potential trialists for your honey?" she asked.

"Yes, I have to make more calls before I go through my correspondence. I'll have letters for you to type, replies, and such."

She returned to her desk.

A tap sounded at the door, and Angus appeared. "Your temporary secretary has arrived," he said, standing aside to gesture at the petite woman behind him.

Niall's gaze snapped to the green-eyed woman sitting at the desk. *What the hell?*

2

PLEASE EXPLAIN

*O*OPS!

"I can explain," Suzie blurted.

Crap, she hadn't thought this escapade through properly because, of course, the real temp would show up. She'd been intrigued, and curiosity was always her downfall.

Stupid. Stupid. *Stupid*.

A quiver ran through Suzie and settled in the pit of her stomach. She'd liked this grumpy man, and discussing business was way better than dealing with amorous shifters. He hadn't studied her like a juicy plum or made her uncomfortable with predatory glances. She gulped.

But he was eyeing her now, and his expression wasn't pretty.

"Who the hell are you?" He rounded his desk and

padded toward her, his expression thunderous.

"Ah, my name is Suzie Paisley. I...ah..." She bobbed to her feet and backed away from the advancing bear shifter. "I'll just be on my way."

"Stop right there."

Suzie attempted a dart to freedom, but the grumpy bear was fast. His fingers wrapped around her upper arm, dragging her to a premature halt. She stumbled against him, the air smacking from her lungs. *"Oomph!"*

"Oh," the woman said from behind them. "Did the agency send someone else? I called to let them know I'd had an accident. They told me this job was urgent, and you were expecting someone immediately."

The bear ignored the woman's prattle and didn't take his attention off Suzie. "Who are you? Who sent you?"

Suzie puffed out a breath. Standing this close to the bear was doing weird things to her libido. He smelled...delicious, like exotic honey with floral and green notes. She shook herself mentally and tried to focus.

Time to spill the truth, even if it sounded farfetched. "My name," she said in a loud and hopefully confident voice, "is Suzie Paisley. I am staying at Castle Glenkirk to take part in the gathering."

The bear kept his gaze on her. Suzie tried to maintain a connection with his thundercloud expression, but the shifter was scary. Her gaze slid down to his feet, shod in shiny black shoes. Big feet to go with the rest of him. Her mind turned a furtive corner, wondering about size in other areas, and heat slid across her face and down her neck. Bloody hell. What was wrong with her?

"Angus, is this woman registered as a gathering participant?" the bear asked, thankfully breaking through her hazy mind.

Suzie paid closer attention.

The tall, spare, gray-haired man wearing a red and black tartan kilt cast his disapproval on her, his piercing blue eyes narrowing as he dissected her appearance. "I'll have to check, but she looks familiar. I recall the Antipodean accent. That group is doing verra well in matches."

Suzie bit her lip, hurt filtering through as her thoughts flicked to Edwina. Since her friend hadn't magically reappeared, every instinct told Suzie their joint plans were no longer viable.

Suck it up, buttercup. She wasn't reliant on her best friend. She could still attend university and study music. Hopefully, Edwina's mate wasn't a tyrant and would let Edwina continue to write music and collaborate.

"Please check," the bear ordered, not taking his gaze off her.

"What about the secretary?" Angus asked.

"Sign her work order so she gets paid and send her home."

Angus ushered the woman away.

The tension ramped up in the office, and Suzie attempted to swallow the nerves threatening her knee stability.

"If what you say is true and you're attending the gathering, why were you wandering around my castle? My private sanctuary." Steel throbbed in the words. Determination to get the truth.

No matter how she answered, her explanation would sound bad. Suzie straightened her black blouse and said, "I don't want a mate, and I'm tired of the gathering activities. I decided to explore."

"By trespassing?"

She couldn't prevent a wince. "I know this looks bad, but I was exploring when you found me. You assumed I was the secretary. Didn't you think it was strange I hadn't reported in with Angus? He escorted the other woman here."

"I assumed Angus had given you directions to my office and you were dawdling." The bear glowered at her, his jaw set like the granite on a Scottish mountain. His lips peeled back, revealing teeth as sharp as hers, and she retreated half a step, every instinct screaming danger.

"Non-disclosure document, remember? No way will I blab about your honey. Not to anyone."

"How can I trust you?"

Indignation rose in Suzie. She was many things, but not a liar. "I'm not a tattle, nor do I gossip."

"You say that, but I have millions at stake." He closed his eyes, a pained expression crossing his face. The flash of emotion had vanished when he focused on her again. "You will stay here, where you can't blab to anyone."

Suzie took another step back. "No."

"Yes."

Suzie gulped and glanced over her shoulder to spot an impassive Angus blocking the sole exit. Her gaze turned back to the bear. His size was intimidating, and his hands looked strong enough to snap her in half without breaking a sweat, even though she wasn't exactly petite. So sue her, but she enjoyed food. A fact her grandmother chided her about at every opportunity.

"Um, don't you think you're overreacting? I spent the morning working without expecting a wage in return." She didn't mention she'd prefer to work the entire day rather than place herself in contact with the mate-seeking shifters. Some had become positively desperate, and witnessing their extreme behavior was sad and off-putting. Not entirely their fault since they faced intense pressure from home.

"Angus will transfer your possessions to this level. You will remain confined."

"What? No!"

He checked his shiny gold watch and frowned. "I have work. You will continue your secretarial duties since the damage is done."

She folded her arms. "You can't make me."

"I can and I will. You pose a danger to my product's future. The business is rife with espionage and other subterfuge. Outright thievery is not uncommon."

"No."

"Angus," the bear said without taking his gaze off her.

"Yes, sir. I'll arrange matters straightaway."

"I'll take her to her room before my scheduled video call."

"Verra, well," Angus said, his head inclining. He retreated and closed the door, clicking it shut.

Suzie blinked, feeling slightly dizzy. Her fertile imagination took over, sailing to cold, drafty dungeons.

"You can't be serious."

The man ignored her protests and towed her from the office like a package, dragging her halfway along the passage before she could dig in her heels or object more strongly.

"Wait. Stop! You can't do this."

The bear was a cone of angry silence. Implacable. Determined.

Temper flared in her then, and she fought, using every bit of her strength. It did no good. The shifter was much stronger than her, scooping her up and draping her over his shoulder with ease. Long, ground-eating strides took him along the passage, although she continued to struggle and curse him. He rounded a corner and bounded to the end of yet another passage without breathing hard.

Suzie's head swam from hanging upside down. She groaned and spat another curse about his parentage as he opened a door and shouldered his way inside. Her head collided with the door jamb, and she saw stars, her cussing turning weak.

He strode into the room and dumped her on the bed.

Suzie gingerly fingered her aching skull. "You can't keep me prisoner. My friends will look for me. They'll worry," she said, glaring at his stony visage.

But none of what she spluttered was the truth. Scott and Liam would think she'd found a mate. They'd scarcely blink because disappearing was what the rest of their friends had done. Anita, Ramsay, Edwina, and now her. Instead of worrying, they'd grumble that they were the last shifters standing.

The bear's dark glower stopped her frenzied thoughts dead. He didn't intend to change his stance. Long strides took him to the door, his black suit trousers hugging his butt and muscular thighs, his white shirt clinging to his strong back.

Suzie cursed under her breath for noticing these stupid details as he exited the room. The solid wooden door shut, trapping her, and she muttered a rude word. That bear had no right to hold her prisoner. She was an innocent bystander who'd helped him out for free. She quashed her guilt at snooping in his private apartments. Yeah, she'd been nosy, so sue her, but she was no industrial spy.

She tried the door. The bastard. It was locked.

She wrenched the handle again, then kicked the door for good measure.

Sharp pain rippled through the soft leather of her slip-on shoe. "Ouch!"

Suzie limped to the double bed and sank down, her head throbbing in sympathy with her abused toe. Her gaze roamed the bedroom, taking in the contents and the avenues of escape. No window exit because she was on an upper floor.

She rose and hobbled to the window. Thick walls transformed the area into a cozy window seat, ideal for reading or mountain gazing. Given the incredible view, this must be one of the castle's towers. Great. Just great. She was a modern Rapunzel, and her hair wasn't adequate if she wanted to escape.

Despondent, she realized she was truly trapped unless... She hustled to investigate the rest of the room. One door opened to a lavish en suite and dressing room.

She caught a glimpse of her face and groaned on seeing a mad woman with hair sticking in all directions. Suzie smoothed it as best she could and wandered back to the main room to continue exploring.

"You idiot," she muttered, feeling her pocket for her phone.

It wasn't there. When had she last seen it?

"Oh," she muttered, sending another silent curse to the heavens. She'd searched for info on honey thefts and must've left it on the desk.

"No phone," she mumbled.

A few frantic moments of searching confirmed there was no phone. However, she discovered a coffee machine and made herself a caramel-flavored coffee. Although she'd been trying to control her sweet cravings and had dropped a few pounds because of her willpower, she opened a container full of shortbread and practically inhaled the first one. The second piece, she savored, enjoying the buttery goodness, despite her dilemma.

The bear couldn't keep her here for long. If she were him, she'd investigate her background. He'd see she wasn't a threat. Her accent had told him she wasn't local, and Angus would confirm her enrolment at the gathering. It would be simple enough for the bear to contact either Saber or London, and they'd tell him she was no honey thief. While she enjoyed the stuff on toast, she was an equal-opportunity girl and liked Vegemite some mornings.

"Huh!" Suzie jumped to her feet and paced the confines

of the tower. It was a beautiful room with a thick carpet in a dove gray underfoot. The curtains and bed covers were in stunning teal and blue-green shades that brought a peacock's feathers to mind and brightened the room.

Under any other circumstances, she'd call herself lucky and wallow in the luxury.

"He'll come to his senses," she muttered, circling the tower again. "Soon."

But he didn't.

Hours passed. Day became night. She made another coffee and ate the rest of the shortbread, even as she hurled curses upon his head.

The next time she saw the bear, she'd attack first and not bother with questions later. She was innocent, dammit, and he had no authority to detain her.

3

A WORKABLE PLAN

NIALL SLAMMED INTO HIS office, furious at himself. He'd taken one look at her, or rather his bear had, and his thinking brain had gone AWOL. So, to counteract this, he'd jumped into grumpy mode and barked orders. Because of his impatience to get started he hadn't given her a chance to explain but had made assumptions.

Now, he had a dilemma.

Yes, she'd signed a non-disclosure document, so he had legal recourse. Yes, she was a damn fine secretary, but none of that mattered if he couldn't trust her.

He dropped into his office chair, the leather squeaking as his body weight distributed. He drummed his fingers on the desktop and tried to fashion a solution for this newest problem.

Bottom line, he couldn't keep her a prisoner at Castle Glenkirk. For one, someone was bound to miss her.

A tap came on the door, and Angus entered. "Sir, I have the information you requested."

"Did she lie about anything?" Niall demanded.

That was a massive no for him. He detested fibs and liars, a remnant from his childhood when his parents and siblings had been economical with the truth. A snarl pushed up his throat, the pain still raw despite the years.

Old history.

He'd escaped the family and their constant taunts. He wasn't that little runt any longer. *A waste of brain space.* Niall redirected his focus to the woman. No problem. His mind trotted straight to her like a tame puppy.

His bear chuffed happily, which surprised Niall. He pictured the woman. She bore pleasing curves. She hadn't been particularly tall, but her green eyes were beautiful. Best of all, she was efficient, confident, and that brain of hers...

Yes, she was an enticing package.

But what did he do with her?

He was so close to releasing his product to the market that he couldn't afford any hiccups.

"Her name is Suzie Paisley, and she comes from Middlemarch in New Zealand. She is a black leopard shifter and a gathering attendee." Angus paused to study the papers he held. "She's one of six from Middlemarch, and three have found partners so far. She and two young men remain."

Niall nodded, his mind busily working through the information. "When is she scheduled to leave?"

"Next Monday," Angus said.

Niall nodded. "Kindly send dinner for two to the dining room." He checked the clock. "In half an hour? Transfer her luggage and belongings to her current bedroom."

Angus dipped his head. "It will be done."

Niall waited for Angus to leave before leaning back in his chair. It groaned beneath his weight, but for once, his thoughts didn't divert to purchasing a new chair. He had a workable plan and looked forward to knocking heads with Ms. Suzie Paisley.

Suzie jerked awake to an abrupt tap on the door. She sprang off the bed and attempted to straighten her wrinkled clothing, her heart jumping with anticipation. If that bear dared to poke his nose into this bedroom, she'd shred him with her claws.

A key turned in the lock, and her muscles tensed as she prepared to spring. She was moving before the door opened and registered precisely who was standing there. The very man. She struck muscle then yelped because the bear was as hard as a rock. His hands snapped out to grasp her forearms and stop her from falling on her arse. Suzie glared at him.

"You have no right to imprison me."

His eyes narrowed. "You're the one who gained access to my office by deception. I have every right to detain you until I can assure myself you're not dangerous to my business."

Suzie's temper cooled a fraction because he was right, dammit. While she hadn't lied to him, she hadn't exactly been truthful either.

"You can't keep me here," she repeated, more for form than anything else because it was evident he could and no one would help her. He possessed her phone, and the tower room was too high, the windows too small for her to shout for aid.

"Come," he said, propelling her from the room.

"Where are you taking me?" She dragged her heels, fear filtering through her bravado. Did the castle have a dungeon? Probably. She'd bet her left arm it'd be full of spiders and other nasties. Probably damp and cold, too.

More time had passed than she realized because the bright sun was sinking toward the horizon. Her stomach gave a complaining grumble, but she didn't pardon herself or otherwise comment. Prisoners got food, didn't they? Dry bread or gruel?

The bear led her through numerous rooms, his pace too quick for her to orientate herself. This castle was a rabbit warren, albeit comfortable and luxurious. She had to admit, whoever decorated had done an excellent job blending old with modern.

Finally, he directed her into a dining room full of a delicious meaty scent.

Suzie's nostrils flared. "You're going to feed me?"

"I thought you might be hungry."

Suzie shot him a glance but didn't let loose her complaints of imprisonment with nothing but shortbread to eat. If she got too lippy, he might return her to that bedroom.

The bear released her arm and pulled out a chair. He jerked his chin with apparent impatience, and she hastened to sit. Seconds later, Angus arrived with a trolley. The additional food scents made her stomach happy, but she was surprised. If he were feeding her, he wouldn't do away with her. Another thought struck. Unless this was her last meal...

"What are your intentions?"

"I thought we'd share dinner and discuss your circumstances," he said in an even tone.

"Oh." She wished Edwina was here because they usually shared trouble. She wanted her best friend. The cliche about curiosity and cats might come true this time. Suzie remained silent while Angus served roast beef, Yorkshire pudding, and a selection of vegetables.

"Gravy?" Angus asked her.

"Yes, please."

"Would you like a glass of wine with your meal?" the bear asked. "I'm having a red."

"Thank you. That sounds nice." Listen to them. So polite. Despite this, Suzie's insides were tied as tightly as her guitar strings. It was the unknown. Exactly what did he intend to do?

The wine was from New Zealand. She noticed the label, and a pang went through her. She missed her family: her parents, younger brother, and sisters.

The bear handed her a glass of the ruby liquid, and she took it, trying not to touch him because that would be awkward. This close, she could smell his bear and the spicy sweetness underlying the animal. She found it strangely unsettling because sitting here at the table with him felt too personal. Her awareness of him had grown,

31

and she noticed little things like his easy way with Angus. She recalled his enthusiasm for honey and the animated discussion of marketing and the process. He loved his business, and his passion for honey was a driving force in his success.

Each layer of this man intrigued her, and she yearned to learn more, to learn everything.

"I don't even know your name," she said.

His gaze lifted to hers, and his lips curled in a charming and wry smile. "I thought you must know, given my initial suspicion was that you were a spy. You truly don't know my name?"

"No." She stared at him, her heart beating immeasurably faster.

"Niall Sinclair."

"I'm sorry to have caused so much trouble for you, Niall." Sincerity came through in her voice, and she meant every word. "Thank you for sharing your dinner with me."

His expression was nonplussed for a fleeting second. He cut a corner off a slice of roast beef and popped it in his mouth. She tried not to notice his capable hands and smooth throat as he swallowed and set down his knife and fork.

"This honey project is significant for me. It is an amazing product and a breakthrough in sports training. I can't afford to let any information slip that might alert the competition. Once my honey hits the shelves, that will be different, but now I need to control every step of production, including who receives information."

"But I understood the gravity of signing a

non-disclosure document, and I certainly can't afford for you to sue me. I'm a student. I put my signature on your paperwork with every intention of keeping my mouth shut. That still applies." She met his gaze and held it. "I am not a dishonest person."

Niall kept his attention on her, his expression serious, and damn if she didn't find that appealing too.

"I called Saber Mitchell and spoke to him."

Suzie straightened abruptly. "You did?"

"Is that a problem?"

"No." She bit her lip. "What did he say?" Did he tell Niall about the mischief she and Edwina had gotten into during their teens? How they'd been in trouble with the police because of their behavior?

"He vouched for your honesty and said you're trustworthy. He also told me you're curious, and your explanation was probably exactly what had happened."

"You believe me now?"

"I haven't decided." Niall started eating again, and Suzie followed suit. "I have a proposal," he said after the silence had continued for several minutes.

"Yes?"

"I need a personal assistant. My last one left to have a baby and doesn't wish to return. I understand her priorities, but it means I require a replacement. A trustworthy one."

"But I'm returning to New Zealand soon. I'm a student, and my university course starts in two weeks."

He cocked his head, interest flitting across his face. "What do you intend to study?"

"My best friend and I applied to study music at the university in Wellington. We both received scholarships." She hesitated before deciding the truth about her family's lack of support would work best. Honesty in all things with this bear. "Neither of our families approve of us studying music, which means we have saved to support ourselves. I'll have to get a part-time job once my course starts to pay for the expenses the scholarship doesn't cover. I have secretarial skills because our families insisted we have a qualification behind us. My parents hoped we'd give up our pursuit of frivolous music, but now that we've done what they wanted, they've run out of ways to stop us." Her thoughts drifted to Edwina. She badly wanted to learn what was happening with her friend. "My friend discovered her mate here at the gathering, so it will be me going to university alone."

"I'm afraid you won't be going either."

"What?" The word escaped and hit screech territory. Her hands clenched her cutlery, and for a second, she was tempted to stab him.

"I want you to stay and work for me until my honey goes to market. You already know a little, and using you as my assistant makes sense instead of hiring a new one or trying to find a temp."

"No. No, I won't do it," Suzie said, the charity she'd been feeling toward Niall detonating in a fiery blaze of anger.

"I'm afraid I must insist."

An implacable tone if ever she heard one. "But your honey isn't hitting the market for another six months.

That was in your notes. You said you wanted to do further tests on the health benefits and structure your marketing before you go public. I start university in *two* weeks. I've worked so hard to get there and jumped over numerous hurdles. Please, don't do this. Don't tear my dreams away from me."

4

Mine!

Niall's gut burned at the pleading in her voice, the yearning in her tone when she spoke of her university course. When he'd talked to Saber Mitchell, he'd told the man the truth. Saber had revealed that Suzie had worked hard to gain her scholarship despite her parents' disapproval. She hadn't attended the gathering to search for a mate, but she'd gone because Saber and his fellow council member had asked her to represent their town.

Niall had been blunt and confessed to Saber Mitchell what his bear had been chanting in his brain since they'd encountered Suzie wandering through his home.

"Mine. Mine. Mine!"

"Yes," Niall said with a tired sigh. "Message received."

The instant attraction to the young woman had thrown him and led to his lack of usual caution. However, he'd asked her to sign the non-disclosure—a point in his favor.

When he'd discovered her nimble brain and efficient work ethos that had knocked him over to his bear's way of thinking.

He'd never imagined encountering a mate and hadn't actively searched. The single shifters who inhabited his castle hadn't enticed him to start an elusive mate hunt. Suzie had crept into his world, and everything had changed.

What he hadn't told her was that he was keeping her not only because of his honey project but also because he feared the problems he'd face with his shifter half if he let her return to New Zealand.

Yeah, he'd told Saber Mitchell the truth and gained the man's grudging approval on the condition he agreed to let Suzie continue her music studies. Niall made a promise, unsure of how to fulfill it.

Now, he rubbed his temples to alleviate the nagging pain that had settled there to plague him. His headaches were many and varied. His honey. Suzie. His promise to Saber Mitchell made in good faith.

"Mine. Mine. Mine!"

"Yes," Nial muttered. "I hear you."

He'd locked Suzie in that room again, feeling bad even though he'd gone ahead. Now guilt trailed him like a bee on a mission.

What the hell was his next move?

He pressed his fingers into the aching spot at his temples.

Saber Mitchell had confided about Suzie's family and their pressure on her to conform. Their expectations for her didn't gel with her dreams and ambitions. Suzie's family was fiercely traditional, and their idea of a dutiful daughter followed their vision for her future. According to Saber, the family's expectations had led to teenager Suzie fighting them every step of the way.

The ache in his head intensified, and his bear restarted his stubborn chanting. "*Mine. Mine. Mine.*"

Niall understood family trouble since he'd struggled with his large, boisterous family from childhood. Because he was the runt, his three older brothers had given him hell. The rest of the family took their cue from his brothers. They bossed him around and tormented him physically and mentally until he'd taken to hiding. His parents had done nothing to stop the bullying. No, they'd expected every cub to fend for themselves. It made their offspring strong.

Once Niall was old enough, he'd relocated from Canada to Scotland. He hadn't heard from his family since and wouldn't trust anyone who did try to contact him.

And this led him back to Suzie.

Could he trust her? Yes, she'd signed papers, but that had never stopped a determined person from making a quick buck. An employee had sold confidential information before, so he was adamant about keeping his new honey under wraps.

"*Mine. Mine. Mine!*"

Niall cursed and pushed the wild, insistent part of his psyche to the back of his mind. He could hardly romance her to their way of thinking when he didn't trust her.

No. This was it. He was out of options. He needed to

keep Suzie at the castle and glued to his side where he could supervise her interactions with others. At this late stage, he couldn't risk anything going wrong. It was everything he'd worked for, the goal he'd striven toward his entire life, and nothing—no one—would mess with him or his honey.

When Niall released Suzie from her room the next morning, he wasn't sure what to expect. His head thumped with the ferocity of a hundred bee stings, and the lack of sleep because of his guilty conscience left him short in the temper department.

"When are you releasing me?"

He noted her packed suitcase sitting by the bed. "Once my honey goes on the market." Niall managed not to snarl, but it was a close-run thing. "Right now, we're heading to the office. I need to work, and you can type my notes for me."

"No."

"Saber mentioned you're a reasonable woman who'd recognize this as the best way to proceed."

The color blanched from her face, leaving her pale, the scarlet slash of lipstick the only color on her face. Even her vibrant green eyes seemed to lose their spark.

"You had a long conversation with Saber?" Disbelief echoed in her words. Shock. A hint of betrayal.

"Yes. I explained everything." Even the fact they were mates. Her shifter half hadn't given her the mate memo yet. Possibly, all the other emotions were muting nature.

"But Saber knows I'm attending university. He and London encouraged us."

"Us?"

"Edwina, my friend. I told you—we were going together, but I haven't heard from her since she left the castle."

"I understand the importance of dreams and goals, and I'm not forcing you to give up your music. Can't you continue your studies remotely or find someone in Britain who can help you study without leaving the castle?"

"No." She folded her arms and glared at him, her luscious mouth set in a firm, mutinous line. "This is kidnapping, pure and simple. You're the one in the wrong. It was your mistake that led me to learn your honey secrets."

Niall barely resisted his wince because every word was accurate. But Saber had told him he understood and appreciated his honesty. He'd given Saber details, or as much as he could, given he didn't know the man, and promised to report back to him weekly. Saber Mitchell had insisted and wanted a video call to see Niall's face.

Niall had conceded to Saber's requests, respecting his determination. It warmed him to know this man cared for his people this much. Suzie was lucky to have this support. Niall wished he'd had a Saber in his background during his youth.

"Suzie," Niall said, striving for patience. Given the threat to his honey, he'd done his best to do the right thing. Bottom line—he didn't know Suzie well enough to believe in her promise. Niall had learned about deception from his family and...

He dragged his mind from the past, angry at himself for slipping into that young, trusting bear's mind. "Work with me or stay locked in this room. Your choice." He strode for the door, and his hand connected with the knob before she spoke.

"I suppose you'll refuse to let me speak to anyone either."

"You can speak to Saber Mitchell." Niall was alarmed to spot the tears in her eyes. With three long strides, he was beside her. His arms went around her quivering shoulders, and he hauled her against his chest. "Ah, lass," he murmured, his nose buried in her hair. "I'm sorry."

She glanced up at him with tear-filled eyes. "You'll let me go home?"

Suspicion rose in him. Were those manufactured tears? "No."

Suzie wrenched away, her glare back in force. She was beautiful. Glorious and a big, fat liar with excellent acting skills.

Niall spun and marched to the door. He departed, securing the lock, and headed to his place of solace. He immersed himself in work, but even then, his deceptive mate hovered at the fringes of his mind.

Niall flung down his pen and cursed. It was kind of ironic that he'd escaped a toxic environment only to fall into the clutches of a mate he couldn't trust. What the hell did he do now?

"Mine. Mine. Mine!" his bear chanted.

"We can't trust her," Niall mumbled.

His bear released an angry growl and continued his litany. Niall studied the clock on his wall and wondered if it was too early to start drinking. He stood and was halfway to his drinks cabinet when his phone rang.

Grateful for the interruption, he retreated to his desk and scooped up his phone. "Sinclair."

"Boss, it's Harris. Someone tried to break into the lab early this morning."

5

A BOSSY CURMUDGEON

SUZIE SPENT A FRUSTRATING morning pacing the luxurious bedroom. Angus had delivered a delicious breakfast and locked the door again once he'd set down the tray. She'd filled an hour lolling in the tub amongst decadently scented bubbles, but her mind refused to divert from the stubborn bear.

Niall Sinclair was driving her crazy. Why did she find him sexy? He was a bad-tempered, bossy, conniving curmudgeon.

It wasn't right for him to keep her prisoner, and she couldn't believe Saber had been okay with this situation.

Saber and London had helped her and Edwina when they'd strayed into stupidity, and representing their town at the gathering was a way of saying thank you for their advice and encouragement. Neither she nor Edwina had hesitated when London explained what they wanted and why. No one had pressured them for positive results, and when she hadn't clicked with anyone, Suzie had been glad. She'd assumed Edwina had the same mindset until her friend abruptly vanished, leaving Suzie with unanswered questions and hurt feelings.

Heavy and hurried footsteps sounded outside her door. The scrape of a key had her whirling. The door burst open, and Niall stood there, fury radiating from his muscular body. "Come with me."

He didn't wait but pivoted abruptly and advanced down the passage. Suzie blinked, her curiosity sparking. She trotted after him, questions trembling on the tip of her tongue. They were in a castle wing she hadn't explored when she caught up. Niall approached a wall, which she belatedly realized was an elevator. Ah! So that was how the castle owner avoided the gathering attendees. Given his preference for privacy and secrets, it was astonishing he'd allow the convention at the castle. She'd guessed he owned it, given he lived in the private rooms above, but maybe that was her assumptions tripping her up again.

"Niall, do you own this castle?"

"What?"

"Do you own Castle Glenkirk?"

"Yes, what of it?" Suspicion colored his tone now.

Disappointment flowed from her in a soft sigh. The man's rough handsomeness and apparent strength were attractive, but his grumpiness was getting old. Who wanted to witness that snarly face every morning?

"I was curious. Why permit the gathering at the castle if it's your home?"

"None of your business. Your job is to assist me until my honey launches. Once that day comes, you're welcome to leave."

"Wow, who rained on your parade?"

"Someone broke into my lab early this morning."

Oh. "Wasn't me. You locked me in the bedroom. I hope you've thought carefully about that. What if there's a fire? I'd burn to a crisp before anyone could rescue me."

The man released a growl, sounding more animal than human, and Suzie bit back her smile. *Excellent. Her prattle was annoying him.* Well, he'd learn how annoying she could be. Soon, he'd be pleading for her to leave. He'd pay her to vacate the premises.

"I know you weren't responsible. You don't have a phone to call anyone."

"Thank you," Suzie said, not hiding her sarcasm. "Where are we going?"

"To my lab. I want to assess the damage." He swung around to nail her with a glare. "Recall you've signed a non-disclosure agreement. If you impart sensitive information to anyone, I *will* sue. You'll rue the day you decided to cross me."

"Well," Suzie said, an understatement of gigantic proportions. "I guess you've told me."

"This isn't a laughing matter." Niall slapped his palms against the stout wooden door leading outdoors, pushing it open.

The early morning sun seared her eyeballs, and she blinked frantically to adjust her sight. She stumbled, and the bear's hand shot out, righting her before her befuddled brain snapped into motion.

He tugged hard. She lurched toward him and collided with his chest. *His hard, muscular chest.* The spring flowers and mint with a hint of honey sweetness she'd come to associate with him assailed her. They stared at each other, and she spotted his bear shyly peeking at her through brown eyes that had turned more amber. Then Niall blinked and thrust her away as if she were something nasty.

Suzie staggered, but he righted her with a quick, steadying hand, leaving her confused. Befuddled. The bear-man didn't behave like other males. While it was true he possessed a little absentminded scientist, the driven businessman was very much in control. That would account for his bad temper, or maybe...

"Do you have a stomachache? Are you eating enough roughage?"

He stared at her briefly before barking, "Stay there while I get the car."

Suzie considered running, but Niall had spoken to Saber. She'd heard the truth in his voice when he'd mentioned this, which meant Saber didn't have concerns for her safety. He would've sent Scott and Liam to rescue her if he'd sensed danger. Saber was supportive like that, and she trusted his instincts. No, she'd stay put as ordered. Despite repulsing him, she was still curious about the bear's next move.

A red sports car zoomed around the corner and braked beside Suzie. She grinned as Niall climbed from the driver's seat and ran around to open the door for her. *Wow, a gentleman.* Those were few and far between. Not even her father did this for her mother, despite their deep affection.

Feeling like a princess, she entered the car and took a deep breath. Delicious bear-man laced with a new-car aroma. Soon, Niall sped down a long driveway away from Castle Glenkirk. Once they reached the village, he took another road which led to a larger town with better transport links.

She'd thought they'd drive right into town, but they were still traveling through green fields studded with cute, shaggy Highland cows when Niall turned onto a side road. He went a short distance, the land becoming hillier before they pulled onto a gravel driveway. When they rounded a corner, a large shed came into view. A muddy hunter-green SUV had parked outside. Niall pulled up beside the vehicle and switched off the ignition. He climbed out and strode to the building's entrance.

When Suzie hesitated, he glanced over his shoulder and backtracked to open her door.

"You're coming with me. Pay attention and take mental notes. I want to hear your thoughts later." He waited impatiently, and she scrambled from the vehicle. The door slammed, then he grasped her arm and propelled her into motion.

He was a mix of complexities and bad moods, keeping her off balance and strangely exhilarated because he wasn't dull, unlike the men she'd dated at home.

"You don't need to drag me," she said when her shorter legs refused to keep up with his long strides. "I'm coming willingly."

He released her arm, and the glower he shot her way warned her to behave. She'd consider this, but all bets were off if he continued acting like a tyrant. She had a limited tolerance for bossy men.

At a side door, Niall plugged in a code and used a key. This opened to a vestibule area with yet more security measures. Niall put his eye to a peephole and waited. After seconds, the lock clicked, and the door opened.

"Wow," Suzie murmured. "You're serious about security. I thought you were taking me to a hay barn."

"That's the idea. Thieves think this is a farm building. They'd never believe we produce honey here."

"But where are your worker vehicles?" Suzie asked. "Surely it takes a team to manufacture the honey?"

"It does, but we use this facility in the pre-production stage. No one knows of it except me, my second-in-charge, Michael, and Harris, who keeps an eye on the place and makes sure everything runs smoothly."

"Have they signed non-disclosure documents?"

"We've worked together since I first arrived in Scotland, and the laird was in charge. We're friends, and I trust them implicitly."

Wow, hard to imagine this grumpy man having friends.

Niall led her along a dimly lit passage into a massive open area partitioned into sections.

"Harris," Niall shouted.

"Over here."

With ground-eating steps, Niall headed toward his friend. Suzie hurried after him, curious about this glimpse into Niall's business. Niall skidded to a halt and released a harsh curse.

A few steps behind him, Suzie took seconds longer to assess the damage. Jars of honey lay on their sides, the liquid contents dripping to the floor. Other jars had broken, shards of glass crushed beneath careless feet. Someone had upended every jar of honey they could find. They'd swept them off shelves, and judging by the smears on the wall, they'd fired jars at every surface.

"So much wasted honey," Niall said, grief flitting across his features along with despair and bitterness.

Suzie glimpsed all these emotions before the big man straightened his shoulders and slid back into businessman mode, laser-focused on the problem and the next steps.

"Did they destroy all the honey?" Niall asked.

"No," Harris said, scraping his hand over his sparse hair. His shoulders were stooped in his wiry frame, but when he glanced at her, Suzie saw bright intelligence in his blue eyes—the curiosity. "The jars we bottled yesterday were in the lunchroom under the table. I ran out of storage, and it's cool in there."

"They didn't trash the lunchroom?" Niall asked, his stark tone alerting Suzie to the importance of the answer. "I left my research notes in there. I meant to grab them, but a phone call distracted me."

"Nay, dinna fash. The room is untouched. None of the honey or your notes were in plain sight." Harris scratched his stubbled jaw, shaking his head. "Instinct told me to store the extra honey in the lunchroom. The alternative was rearranging out here to create more room, so at least some is safe. Should I call Michael and get him to help with clean up?"

"Yeah, good idea. What about our production details?"

"They're here, but I'm wondering if someone photographed or copied them because they weren't how we left them." Harris's voice turned grim. "Laddie, we'll need to bring forward our release date. It's the only way to get a jump on our competitors."

"Aye," Niall said. "This is Suzie. She's helping with paperwork and marketing."

Harris frowned, opened his mouth, and shut it again as if he'd thought better of what he'd intended to say. He pulled out his phone. "I'll call Michael."

But instead of jumping straight into action, the two men stared at the havoc for a moment longer and shared a loaded glance. Along with the anger pouring off them came a dispirited air.

Right. She could fix that by shifting frustration into activity. "How did the intruders enter the building?" Suzie asked. "From observation, security is tight."

"As far as I can ascertain, they climbed onto the roof and cut their way inside," Harris said.

"We'd better clear the mess and determine what equipment to replace. I'll organize extra security to monitor the building," Niall said.

Suzie was pleased he'd lost his frozen shock. "What can I do? Should I start picking up broken jars? Do you have a box to toss them into?"

Harris sent her a grateful look. "I'll get you a bin and a pair of gloves to protect your hands." He rushed away, leaving her with a brooding Niall.

"Do you have any suspects?" she asked.

Niall gave an irritable shrug. "Honey production is a cut-throat yet profitable business. It could be any of my competitors. Once we reached the testing stage, anyone might've spoken out of turn despite promising non-disclosure."

"It could've been worse," Suzie said. "At least Harris saved a few jars of honey."

"Yes, but they've probably taken jars to analyze along with our production notes," Niall said.

"Some of your new honey?"

An amused snort escaped him. "I hid it beneath a stack of research books. If they didn't notice the other honey, they won't have our new product."

"A bonus."

"This is bad enough. Our notes and other newer products will give our competitors an advantage."

Suzie hated seeing the disillusionment, the traces of bitterness. She thought she might have to cope with a sulky male, but he shrugged off the emotions riding him and set about righting equipment and taking stock of the damage.

Suzie worked at his side, tossing broken glass into a box and other items into a rubbish sack. Harris toiled with them.

"Harris? Niall?" a masculine voice called.

The new arrival rounded the corner and came to an abrupt halt. He cursed before closing the distance between Harris and Niall and having an animated discussion.

Suzie continued working until her back started protesting, and when she checked her watch, she was surprised two hours had passed. Although they hadn't chattered, she'd enjoyed working with the men to right the damage and get them underway with their secret tests again.

Harris arrived with a tea tray, and Niall and the newcomer followed him, their easy conversation and verbal shorthand telling of a long-standing friendship. Harris poured mugs of strong tea and handed out pieces of buttery shortbread.

"Michael, this is Suzie, my new office assistant," Niall said.

Suzie caught the surprise in the brown eyes before the man of her height offered his hand. His smooth palm collided with hers briefly before he released her. Suzie bit back her grimace, deducing from his expression that he thought she and Niall were lovers. Ugh to sweaty hands and insincere handshakes.

"Pleased to meet you," Suzie said, flashing a half-hearted smile. Some people made the worst assumptions.

He dipped his head before asking Niall a question. Suzie concentrated on the excellent shortbread and her tea before starting work again.

It was another hour before the room appeared orderly, albeit absent of equipment.

"I've arranged for security guards around the clock," Niall told Harris and Michael. "Make sure they know who you are. Introduce yourself before you leave for the night."

"I will," Harris promised.

Michael nodded. "I'm heading back to the plant now, but I'll drop by in the morning."

"Thanks." Niall strode halfway along the passage, with her trotting behind like a pet dog before he came to an abrupt halt. "Wait here."

He retraced his path and disappeared into the room they'd come from. Suzie heard him speak with Harris but couldn't interpret the words. When Niall returned, he carried a box and a red folder. He strode past her without a word, and with a roll of her eyes, she fell in behind.

"Ah, the security men have arrived." He placed the box and folder in the trunk. "Stay here."

"Yes, sir," she muttered, grumpy, until her gaze lit on his rear end. Nice. The bear did have an attractive body, even if his scowl spoiled his appearance. But that accent... It canceled out some of his bad points. She grinned but wiped her expression clean when he stomped back, having spoken with the security team.

"What now?" she asked.

"We return to the castle."

Enlightening, not. "Did the thieves get any of your new wonder honey?"

"Not the final product we intend to market. The thieves got earlier iterations and notes. The honey Harris stored in the lunchroom was a different blend but still valuable. We got lucky, and someone interrupted our thieves, or they thought they'd found all the honey."

"Will the security guards be enough?"

"Fingers crossed," Niall said drily. "I can work from the castle, if necessary, in my small lab there. I'll get you to collate the test results that have come in so far. Next, we'll decide on the label and jar and organize shipping." He tapped his fingers as he snapped out instructions. "We'll have to hire guards to protect the shipments and ensure the honey goes on sale immediately. I want you to write up an advertising proposal. We're cutting it fine on promotion, but pre-booking can lead to competitor leaks."

"But I'm flying home soon."

"No," Niall snapped. "Since you inserted yourself into my world, you're staying and seeing this out. You can go home in six months. No more discussion."

Suzie planted her hands on her hips, her fury hot and instant. "For the umpteenth time. You can't make me stay. That is kidnapping, imprisonment, and dozens of other charges."

Niall scowled at her. "I have your passport."

Suzie spluttered before her teeth snapped together. "Saber didn't agree to that."

"Call him and ask." Niall's confident tone told her everything. He wasn't lying because he had spoken to Saber. She frowned. Maybe it was Saber teaching her a lesson.

Niall could hold her here but not constantly watch her. Let him try.

6

UNWELCOME VISITORS

B ACK IN HIS CASTLE office, Nial unpacked his honey
samples and the notes he'd brought for safekeeping.
His mind drifted to Suzie—the annoying woman his bear
craved and didn't want to leave. There had been women
in his past, but none had affected him this way. She kept
interrupting his thoughts when he was trying to work,
mucking up his efficiency and logical mind.

She'd asked if she could go for a walk—a reasonable
request, but he'd had things he wanted to do. So he'd sent a
trusted employee with her with strict instructions for him
not to let her out of his sight. The problem—he'd noted
the hint of appreciation in the wolf shifter's gaze. He'd
kept everything together until the pair had left. *Barely*.

"*Mine. Mine. Mine!*" his bear chanted, the litany
growing wearisome.

"She is staying for six months," Niall muttered, praying

that his bear would get over his infatuation with the leopard shifter.

He'd considered marriage, but when the idea occurred, it was because he was thinking of children and passing on the legacy he'd inherited and built upon. He'd thought to look among the daughters of his business associates. Human or not, the choice of a wife hadn't mattered. His bear had never asserted his opinion before.

Niall stalked to the window and glanced out at the private garden below. His gaze went straight to Suzie. The sun glinted off her hair, and she laughed at something her escort said. A low growl rumbled up his throat, and a burning sensation darted through his chest. He knuckled his breastbone to ease the pain while his gaze followed the pair through the garden.

"*Mine!*" his bear chanted.

Niall cursed and dragged himself away. He was ten years older than her, and her cheerful chatter would drive him crazy. By the time six months had passed, they'd be heartily sick of each other.

His phone rang, and glad of the interruption, Nial plucked it off his desk. "Sinclair."

"Sir, it's Robbie at the gatehouse. Two men to see you. They say they're your brothers."

Niall's hand tightened on the phone, but he controlled the curse that tickled the tip of his tongue. "Did they give you names?"

"I shall inquire," Robbie said.

Something told Niall he'd already asked and that the men had declined to give their names. If it were his brothers, they'd be up to their usual games. He mightn't have seen them for almost twenty years, but he hadn't tried to hide despite traveling to a different country. His entire family were bullies and freeloaders and always took the easy way. Mostly, stealing or intimidation, and as the runt, he'd taken their abuse.

Hell, had his brothers broken into his property?

Robbie came back. "They say their names are Euan and Colin."

A growl crawled up his throat, his bear as perturbed as him. Their timing was certainly suspicious. "Tell my brothers," he said in an icy voice, "they are not welcome here, and I have no wish to see them. They made their feelings very clear before I left home. Nothing has changed."

"Yes, sir." Robbie's crisp acceptance released the tension seeping into Niall's shoulders.

Niall pocketed his phone and resumed his position at the window. He sought Suzie and found her sitting on a bench with her face turned to the sun. Her escort was nearby and fiddling with his phone, his attention split between Suzie and his screen.

Niall returned to his desk, intending to go through his plan again to tweak and perfect, given the destruction of some of their product, but his mind refused to settle. His brothers' arrival. Why? Why did they seek him after all these years? Knowing them, they wouldn't have cared about his disappearance—one less mouth to feed.

Maybe he should've spoken to them.

No. He'd survived—no—thrived without his family to

drag him down.

The door to his office flew open, and Suzie stalked inside.

"I strongly disagree but will stay. I'll work for you without further protest. You will pay me a fair wage and give me time off. You'll let me go into the village if I want, and you will pay for a music course so I won't lose six months. I love my music and refuse to give it up. Do we have a deal?"

Niall dissected her expression while his mind worked the angles and requests she'd asked of him. He'd already promised Saber he'd help with her music. "Give me a list of the music courses you'd like to take. Yes, it's only fair to receive remuneration. Yes, you can go to the village. Check with the pastor because they sometimes have musical concerts and recitals at the church. If you have any problems, please ask me, and we'll have a reasonable discussion. Is that agreeable with you?"

Suzie wore a frown but nodded. "I'll trust you, but no funny stuff. Secretarial duties and nothing else."

"I understand." Niall winced when his bear started chanting. On the plus side, only he could hear the annoying protest. "I might require your presence at functions. Business dinners and a charity ball. Is that acceptable?"

Suzie thrust out her hand. "We have a deal."

"Excellent. I want to review my strategy for the honey's release and decide on a name and label."

They spent an enjoyable three hours refining Niall's plan. Enjoyable for him. Working with an intelligent woman made him incredibly happy. His bear was happy. He was happy. The plan was a winner. He felt it in his gut, and part of that confidence came from the ideas they'd sparked together by imagining what if. Exciting spins on the traditional that he thought would grab the public's attention. Once they tasted his honey, he was confident it would sell itself.

Angus had sent sandwiches and coffee from the kitchen, but now it was late afternoon. Niall glanced at Suzie and wondered if she'd like to take a forest walk with him. His bear sighed happily, and Niall verbalized the idea before analyzing the pluses and minuses.

"I could use some fresh air," he said. "Would you like to walk in the woods with me?" Niall cringed. That sounded like a corny pickup line. A walk. *Huh!*

But to his relief, she beamed.

"I would love that. Do I have time to change into shorts? It's such a lovely day." She paused. "Or will we run in our animal forms?"

"*Mine. Mine. Mine!*" his bear chanted.

Niall's heart leaped because that sounded like heaven. He'd love to see her feline in person, but no, he could make do with her bare legs. Shifting wasn't possible since humans walked and rode their bikes along the paths. "That sounds lovely, but not this time. The woods are a shared one. I like to walk there because the bluebells bloom in the spring. It's a lovely sight."

She grinned, and his bear released a loud sigh. Loud enough to make her blink.

Heat invaded Niall's cheeks, a novelty since nothing

threw him. "My bear," he said, avoiding Suzie's gaze, then giving in to his need to see her reaction. "He loves the woods. Sometimes, I'll go at night when shifting is safer."

"It sounds delightful, and I'd love to go for a walk. I exercise often at home. My friend and I take exercise classes with Isabella, and she's a hard taskmaster."

"I'll rendezvous with you at the elevator in ten minutes. Is that long enough?" he asked, praying she wasn't a woman who preened for hours.

"Ten minutes is plenty of time," Suzie said.

Niall took his time, changing from his suit into a more casual polo shirt and shorts with old and comfortable boat shoes on his feet.

Suzie was waiting when he arrived, and he braced for his bear's habitual chant. Instead, a lustful sigh echoed through his mind. Yeah, that was something he and his bear could agree on. While Suzie was of average height, she had gorgeous, toned legs. His palms tingled with the urge to touch.

Instead, he placed his hand on the small of her back and urged her forward, his nose twitching at her enticing scent. She wore white shorts and a green blouse that matched the color of her eyes. She'd tied her hair back in a high ponytail and wore sensible shoes. Not the spiked heels one of his past girlfriends had worn to walk in the woods. She'd shrieked on seeing a squirrel, and their date had gone downhill from there.

Niall ushered Suzie into his car, and they drove through the village to the wilderness.

"I love the village," Suzie said. "It's like the traditional

English towns I imagined before arriving. Your castle is beautiful, too. How did you come to own it?"

The question took Niall back to when he'd first arrived in Scotland. He'd scrimped and saved to get the airfare. He'd recognized the move would be difficult, but he'd also known his family would suck him dry if he stayed. The bullying he could take, but Niall refused to sink to their level. They lived by conducting scams and outright thievery, and each of his older brothers and sisters thought of him as weak because he'd wanted to go to school and learn. His breaking point had come when he'd met a girl he liked a lot. They'd been dating for six months when his brothers—Euan and Colin—had come across them at a cafe. At first, their appearance had alarmed him, but his brothers had acted charming. That should've warned him for a start. Instead, he'd been grateful his brothers weren't treating him like crap. Millicent—his girlfriend—had told him his brothers were lovely.

He hadn't discovered until it was too late that Euan and Colin had followed them when he'd escorted her home. They'd arranged meetings that had seemed casual to Millicent. She'd mentioned running into them at the market, but he had thought little of it. Later, when he'd examined the past, it had been a big blaring sign he shouldn't have missed. Either Euan or Colin or hell, knowing his brothers, both had seduced Millicent. They'd dragged her into their world of booze and drugs, and despite him warning her, she'd gone willingly.

The blazing row they'd had before they'd broken up had stunned him. It had destroyed him because he and his bear had cared for her, even though she was human and unaware of his world. Euan and Colin had taken care of that. They'd blasted away her rose-colored glasses and dragged her into the chaos. Not that she'd argued much from what Niall had witnessed. Six months later, Millicent had died in a motor vehicle accident, but the designer drugs and booze had already done the damage.

The Millicent he had known had vanished.

Niall slid a glance at Suzie. Millicent hadn't been his mate, but he'd liked her a lot, and his brother's malicious seduction had torn him apart. He had problems with trust now. He understood that and owned it. His brothers' actions and Millicent's defection had been the last push required to get him to summon his bravery and leave. A new life. One where he made decisions and took responsibility for them. One where he didn't have a family. One where people respected him because of his achievements.

And now Euan and Colin had made an unexpected appearance, their timing impeccable and enough to set his warning antenna blaring, especially with the invasion of his property.

He forced himself to smile, and Suzie smiled back with warmth and openness, even after how he'd treated her. Guilt tangoed in his gut and echoed in his mind.

"*Mine. Mine. Mine!*" The chant sounded so demanding that part of him wondered if it had been audible to Suzie. When she didn't react, his grip on the wheel eased.

"The castle," she prompted.

"I inherited it," he said, pushing aside the memories crowding his mind.

"You did?" Lively curiosity pooled in her expression.

"An elderly man owned the castle. I answered an advertisement for a gardening job. He was a cranky old bachelor, but he saw something in me. His hobby was making honey, and since I'm a bear, I have a greater-than-normal interest in the substance. I found the process interesting and had a knack for it. I enjoyed working in the gardens and learning about the different plants. He gave me the use of a cottage, and our friendship started from there. He was a bit of a curmudgeon." Niall felt the smile that curved his lips. Cameron Glenkirk had possessed a cranky demeanor. He'd been a lonely man, while Niall had hungered for any relationship not tainted by his family or his association with them.

"We were an unlikely pair, but I lived and worked here for almost six years before Cameron died. He left me and Angus everything, along with a decent amount of money. We'd always talked about upping our honey production but hadn't done more than sell it at local markets and a stall at the gate. After Cameron died, I made it my mission to make his dream come true."

"Wow," Suzie said. "That is amazing. Did you know he intended to leave you the castle?"

"No, it was a hell of a shock. I would've panicked if Cameron had told me before his death. He left me a letter explaining everything and telling me what he hoped for my future and our honey. His belief helped me steady my nerves and plan. He'd enjoy hearing about the castle rental and the honey's success. According to Cameron, the place lacked vitality and people.

"You should call your new honey after him," Suzie said. "Call it Cameron's Gold or something similar. Honey, unlike wine, lacks a name. Give it a vintage and a personalized name. Make it special. And if you experiment in the future with different varieties of the same, you could give them associated names."

Excitement burst in Niall. "That's an excellent idea. We'll brainstorm names later." He didn't want this outing to end. "Why don't we have an early dinner at the local pub?"

"I'd enjoy that. I've fallen in love with their steak and kidney pie," Suzie said.

Niall pulled up in the gravel lot and parked. "I'm glad I thought of this. It's been too long since I walked for the pleasure of it and enjoyed the forest." He climbed out of the car and hot-footed it to the passenger side. Suzie had already opened the door, but he waited for her to descend before locking the vehicle with the remote.

Suzie inhaled, her expression relaxed and a gentle smile playing on her lips. "Are the bluebells finished blooming?"

"We might sight a stray flower, but a spring visit displays the full beauty of the spectacle."

"Is there much wildlife around?"

"Squirrels and the occasional badger. Most of the shifters here are wolves and run on their private lands. This area has too many wandering humans to appeal to shifters."

"Where do you go when you shift?"

"I'm lucky to have hundreds of acres attached to the castle property. With me, it's more a problem of finding the time to shift because I'm busy. Lots of balls to juggle."

"Is that why you're cranky? You don't let your bear out to play."

Niall spluttered while his bear preened like a giddy child. "*Mine,*" he said in a firm voice. Niall needed a shift of subject before his bear pushed him into embarrassment. He hated to disappoint this woman. No, he wanted to impress her, a sentiment he hadn't felt since Millicent.

"Tell me about Middlemarch," he said. "Saber Mitchell intrigued me during our talk. I thought he might declare war on me for ah..."

"Kidnapping me? Holding me captive?" she asked in a deceptively sweet voice.

"Hmm," he said, neither agreeing nor disagreeing.

"Middlemarch is a small country town. When I was young, it was all black leopard shifters living secretly among the humans. Since Saber Mitchell became head of the council, things have changed. Wolves have moved into Middlemarch, but there is no animosity between the two species. We participate in the same events and work toward making Middlemarch a great town."

"I'd never heard of the place."

"It is small."

The gravel and leaves crunched under their feet as they entered the welcome shade of the forest. Oak and birch trees allowed dappled sunlight to reach the forest floor. Niall sucked in a deep breath and savored the crisp air tinted with greenery and bark. He caught a hint of deer musk, and a squirrel ran out on a branch above them, chittering at the interruption.

"I can see why you enjoy it here. It's peaceful and beautiful."

Niall smiled, the curve of his lips surprising him because he didn't display his emotions. His bear made a humming sound of approval. She'd passed his test.

"Will you show me where the bluebells grow? So I can imagine them in bloom?"

Niall gazed at her, then nodded. That was the moment he gave in to his bear's urgings, although if he was honest, he'd liked her from the moment he'd found her studying the portraits on the wall in his castle. Her grasp of business matters and interest in his honey had deepened his awareness and added respect to the equation. On impulse, he reached out and took her hand. To his delight, she didn't pull away but continued to walk at his side.

"What else do you do when you're not working?" she asked.

"I enjoy music, but I have an awful singing voice. Any outdoor activity is fun because I spend so much time working. If I'm traveling, I try hiking, into the wilderness, or exploring the honey in the area."

"Music is my passion," Suzie said. "I can sing, and Edwina and I write songs together."

"What genre?" Niall asked, interested in learning everything about this fascinating woman. Yeah, he'd given up arguing with his bear, beginning to think his shifter half was one hundred percent right.

Suzie Paisley was their woman.

The sharp crack of a stick on the path behind them had them freezing and exchanging glances. Niall scanned the trees, seeing nothing but every sense telling him they were in danger.

"Down," he snapped seconds before a sharp balloon-popping sound came to him. Something struck the tree branch inches above their heads.

7

DINNER FOR TWO

"**W**HY ARE THEY SHOOTING at us?" Suzie demanded. "Didn't they check their target first? These idiots shouldn't get away with endangering innocent hikers."

They crouched behind a broad tree trunk, wide enough to screen their bodies. Suzie peered through the undergrowth, straining to catch every sound. Niall had his phone out and was speaking with the local police.

"Stay where you are," the cop instructed.

Niall gave him directions for their location and hung up after telling the policeman they'd heard one shot.

"Accident or not?" Suzie asked. "Something to do with your honey?"

"The gossip vine is silent, which is unusual. As far as I know, everyone testing the honey for me has adhered to my privacy conditions."

"What about the break-in at your property?"

"Good point. We reported the crime to the police, but I'll mention it." He scowled, the harsh lines digging into his cheeks a testament to his anger. His unease. "It seems strange for someone to go to so much trouble. The theft of our samples is more understandable. I can't believe anyone would shoot at us on purpose."

"Stranger things have happened," Suzie said. "Greed is a powerful emotion."

Voices carried to them, and Suzie glanced at Niall. "That can't be the police. I doubt they're this fast."

The voices came closer. Niall slowly stood and peered around the tree trunk while Suzie craned her neck to see before rising when four teenagers came into view. Three girls and one guy. The male caught sight of them first, his startled expression giving way to sly humor. He nudged the girl closest to him and murmured something too faint for Suzie to hear. She had a great imagination, though, and her cheeks flamed.

The four walked past, their muffled whispers and laughter continuing until they were out of sight.

"Well," Niall said, plucking two leaves off Suzie's hair. "I can guess what they're thinking."

"Yeah, exactly what I would've assumed at their age." Suzie straightened her rumpled clothes, part of her wishing that she had been rolling around with Niall.

A masculine shout interrupted their chuckles, and a man in a policeman's uniform approached them.

"Mr. Sinclair?" he asked.

"Yes," Niall said. "You were quick."

"I was a few streets away," the cop said. "You reported gunfire?"

"We believe the hunter has left because a group of teens just walked past." He gestured toward the tree. "You'll find the bullet lodged in the trunk. It nearly hit us."

"One shot?" the policeman asked.

"That's right," Niall said. "It's possible the four teenagers scared them away, or they were embarrassed when they realized they'd targeted people instead of animals."

"The no-hunting signs are prominent," the policeman said, sounding slightly harried when his radio squawked insistently. "I'll dig the bullet out, search for shell casings, and if the idiot shoots again in this area, we'll have evidence to tie him to this incident." He paused. "Assuming we can catch him."

"Thank you," Niall said, his forehead scrunched in a frown. "Someone broke into one of my properties early this morning. I've reported the incident," he told the cop.

His stillness and the faint thread of worry told her he didn't think this was a mere hunter. He *did* suspect it had something to do with his honey production and had ties to the earlier incident.

"This morning? I'll speak to the person in charge. Please stop by the station to give statements." The policeman glanced at her before turning to Niall. "You know where we are. Please don't forget. If the hunter shoots here again, we need ample evidence to charge him."

"Is tomorrow morning soon enough?" Niall asked. "We intended to go for dinner."

70

"That's fine." The policeman nodded to two adults who walked past with their two young children. He turned back to Niall, wincing at the spate of police codes squawking through his radio. "Looks as if school is out. Take care."

"Thank you." Niall took her elbow and led her back to the path. "Do you want to keep walking, or would you like to return to the castle?"

"More walking," Suzie said without hesitation. She waited until they were out of earshot. "You think someone targeted us."

He exhaled, the sound floating heavily in the air. "Yes. Given the number of people walking this path now, it should be safe enough. It won't be as romantic and peaceful, but the scenery and fresh air are an incentive to continue."

"You surprise me." A smile flirted with her lips and gained control.

His brows rose, his hazel eyes glinting with amusement. "You think I don't have any romance game because I'm a grumpy bear?"

"I didn't think you'd talk openly about intimacy," Suzie said, not hiding her surprise. "Most guys don't. In my experience."

"Cameron once gave me advice on courting women. His counsel—I'd make an excellent husband and father if I stood out from the other men." Niall smiled at the memory, and it softened the stern lines of his visage. "According to Cameron, I have a grouchy expression, which makes people shy away. He told me my enthusiasm shines when I'm interested in a topic, and that's a good look for me. He also suggested if I wanted to find a wife, I shouldn't hide my true self. Cameron told me I was a romantic and should never conceal my tendencies from someone I cared for since honesty was an asset." He ceased talking and grinned at her. Grinned. The stern lines on his face relaxed, his hazel eyes sparkled, and Suzie's heart did a rapid pitter-patter. Wow. If he chose, the man had game.

Suzie swallowed hard, feeling the heat on her cheeks. She'd had boyfriends before, but did Niall mean he was interested in her as a close friend rather than her expertise in the office? She was afraid to ask.

However, she needed to know for her peace. "Are you telling me I'm not just a secretary?"

He snorted. "With your forceful personality?" Niall halted and reached for her hand. "Let me remove the guesswork for you."

Puzzled, she stared at him, but he said nothing else. He tugged her closer and let his hands slip up her arms to rest on her shoulders. He grinned down at her, and once again, his grin had her pulse racing. The man was imposing and driven. It was how he ran his business and became successful. She liked that about him, admired his business acumen, but this part of the bear was charming and delightful.

Unexpected.

Before Suzie could wonder at this previously hidden facet, he tilted her head and stared into her eyes. She glimpsed a hint of otherness—his bear—before his lips touched hers in a tentative kiss. The restraint didn't last for long. Startled, she gasped, and Niall took advantage, deepening the kiss and infusing passion.

Suzie gripped Niall's shoulders, hanging on for dear life because this kiss knocked her equilibrium. Her knees wilted like spaghetti noodles while her feline half basked in approval of her actions. *Yes, let the bear kiss you. Touch you.* Heck, her feline self wanted to roll onto her back and show her belly.

When Niall drew back, Suzie gaped wordlessly, her mouth tingling. The men—boys—she'd dated and allowed touching privileges had been nothing, a mere blip on her radar, compared to Niall's kiss.

She contemplated saying something intelligent and humorous, but her brain let her down, and all that emerged was a breathy "Wow."

"Exactly," Niall said, stepping back but holding her right hand. "My bear wanted you from the moment we saw you. It's a wonder you haven't heard his demands."

"Really?" She swallowed hard before she spoke but wanted to give him honesty. "You're an attractive male, but until now, my feline has indicated nothing either way."

"And now?"

"She's interested. So am I."

"It's nothing to do with my wealth."

"I'm too blissed out to be insulted. That is for you to judge. You're the one who'll have to decide if I'm a gold-digger or something worse. But I want to remind you I intend to return to New Zealand. I'm happy to do that if you'll let me go."

"No." The sound was sharp and held possessiveness.

"Let's take this time to become acquainted. I like you, Suzie, and I don't say that lightly. I haven't met a woman who challenges me like you, and I enjoy your company, whether we're walking in the forest or working on an element of my honey business. If I was to search, I doubt I could find anyone who suited me so well. So please tell me you will stay of your own free will. See where this magic between us might go."

Suzie stared at him, her mouth agape and her eyes wide. This man was asking instead of ordering her or forcing her to accede to his wishes. She narrowed her eyes, her brain working through the pros and cons. She'd wanted to go to university so badly, but Edwina's absence would take the shine off the achievement. If she could... "You truly intend to pay me for my work?"

"Fair wages plus a bonus if we get the honey to market on time."

"And I'll stay at the castle?" She wanted this doubly confirmed.

"Feel free to use the current room and come and go at your leisure."

"Can I spend time with my friends? The two remaining ones left from our original group."

"You're welcome to invite them to visit for dinner, but you mustn't tell them about the honey. Just tell them enough to get them to stop asking questions."

A sneaky thought occurred, and she wondered if he would balk at her suggestion. "What if I told them you were my mate?" She now suspected this was the truth, and the gathering was a brilliant cover. Not one shifter would mention it to a human.

Niall met her gaze, and she glimpsed his bear in the gold swirl that suddenly dominated his eyes. A slow smile crept across his face, spellbinding in its charm. It transformed him from a grumpy bear to a sexy shifter who'd attract any woman's attention.

"I might enjoy that," he said in a sexy rumble.

Her mouth dropped open, and she pressed her lips together once she realized. "You would?"

"I've confessed already. I like you a lot. You're intelligent, excellent at your job, and you don't bore me with your prattle."

Suzie rolled her eyes. "Thanks, I think."

He grinned, and her breath caught. He looked much younger and more carefree when he cast away his serious side. "Also, I enjoy looking at you. Plus, you aren't afraid of my temper."

"Okay."

Niall pulled up in the parking lot for a pub Suzie hadn't yet visited—The Black Bull. Once out of the vehicle, she snapped a shot of the pub sign depicting a snorting black bull. Fields sat on one side of the pub, full of contented Highland cattle chewing their cud. Suzie skipped in that direction and took a photo to send to her father. A cattle farmer, he'd enjoy seeing the hairy, horned beasts.

Niall waited patiently, leaning casually against the hood of his vehicle. A tiny smile played on his lips, and she had the strange desire to touch him or at least run her finger over his mouth and test it for softness. She had the oddest feeling that this man used his grumpiness as a barrier, and he was marshmallow-soft inside. She was seeing a side of him that most didn't.

"Are you done?" he asked.

"For now." She savored the touch of his hand on the small of her back as he pushed open the double front doors and showed her into the dimly lit pub. The floor was wooden underfoot, with several standing tables and eight tables with chairs to the right.

"Grab a table while I get us a drink," Niall said. "What would you like?"

"I'm working my way through the local gins, so I'll take a gin and tonic, please. Something with botanicals."

Niall returned five minutes later with a pink gin and tonic, a beer for him, and two bags of crisps. "The kitchen is closed for another hour."

Suzie nodded and took a sip of her drink. "Nice," she said. "Is it a local one?"

"Made in Edinburgh, according to the barman." Niall's gaze went past her to the door, and he snapped out a curse.

Suzie half turned in her seat, but Niall's hand shot out to stay her.

"No," he said in an undertone. "Perhaps they won't notice us." He cursed again.

Suzie set down her drink and reached for a packet of crisps. The tension in Niall spread to her, and a bolt of apprehension shot through her when she saw the smile on Niall's mouth—the one that didn't reach his eyes. Whoever he'd spotted had knocked him off balance. She could practically feel his bear vibrating beneath his skin, which set her feline on edge. She tugged at the top of the crisp pack, exerted too much force, and spilled crisps across the table.

"Sorry," she whispered.

"Niall," a masculine voice said, the owner halting behind her. "Fancy seeing you here."

Something about the smug note in the voice raised her hackles. Intuition told her this man had known their location. Did that mean he'd followed them from the castle? Had he shot at them? Her gut cried yes, and Suzie had learned to trust her instincts. Her mother knew stuff, too, although their grandmother—her father's mother—dismissed this freaky power out of hand.

"Who is the pretty lady?" a second masculine voice asked.

Suzie's stomach flipped, but she plucked a crisp from the packet and popped it into her mouth. Niall tensed even more until he reminded her of a coiled spring. Whoever these men were, Niall loathed them. She could see it in the hard glint of his eyes.

"Aren't you going to say anything, baby brother?" the first voice said, its taunting quality irking Suzie. "Introduce us to your friend."

She hated bullies. Especially now since hindsight told her she and Edwina had started to tread this path. That of a thug. She hadn't liked what she'd seen and thought she'd become a better person. She'd certainly tried. And she recalled the pain in Niall's voice when he'd told her about his family and their cruel treatment.

Suzie picked up her drink and savored the botanical notes of the gin as she swallowed. Summer fruits, juniper, and herbs. She'd quiz the barman later and see how good she was at distinguishing the flavors.

"Hey, Runt. You don't seem pleased to see us. Afraid we're gonna steal your lady friend? Or did you pay for her company?"

Suzie's breath hissed through her teeth, and she opened her mouth to fire a reprimand.

Niall beat her to it. "That's enough. What is so important that you must hound me? Whatever you want, spit it out and leave."

"What about the niceties that you're always harping about?" one brother asked.

"Quit mucking around," Niall snapped. "What. Do. You. Want?" Fury glittered in his expression. His bear was mighty pissed, as evidenced by the amber flecks in Niall's hazel irises.

One brother edged around the table and into Suzie's sightline. He matched Niall's height, and she could see the resemblance in the eyes and cheekbones. Handsome in a hard way, he bore a scar that ran from his ear to the corner of his mouth. He'd slicked his hair back with something that darkened the color to muddy brown and wore a thick gold chain around his neck. This was the sort of man her grandmother had warned her about. One she might've flirted with once but now sensed was trouble. Niall was worth ten of him.

Suzie wanted to tell Niall and his brother that, but she remained mute. She and Niall could talk later.

The second brother appeared, his smirk provoking her urge to strike. They thought Niall would capitulate and do whatever they wanted.

Niall pulled out his phone. "Tell me what you want, or I'll contact the police and tell them you're the ones who were shooting at us in the forest."

8

VISITORS FROM THE PAST

NIALL HELD HIMSELF STILL, fighting his bear's orders to attack. His brothers were up to no good and hadn't denied his charges. He grabbed the business card the cop had given him from his wallet and started pushing buttons.

"What are you doing?" Colin's eyes were wide and held a trace of shock.

Niall didn't allow himself to indulge in petty satisfaction. He went for the jugular. "Calling the cops."

"Knock it off," Euan snapped. "Family don't turn their brothers into the cops."

"Even if they took potshots at innocent people out for a relaxing walk?" Niall asked, his tone calm, even while his bear bucked at his iron control. The more Niall thought about it, the more his conviction grew. He was right. His older brothers wanted something from him. He changed tack, again going for direct. "What do you want?"

Euan shot a glance at Suzie. She stared coolly back, her expression not changing, even when Euan leered at her.

Enough! "What *do* you want?"

"We want to speak with you in private."

"Yet you approach me in a pub." Niall didn't bother hiding his sarcasm. And he realized something else. During the years apart from his family, he'd grown and acquired balance when it came to his brothers.

They were ruffians, and if he let them, they'd walk all over him.

Not happening.

"You wouldn't speak to us at that castle," Colin said.

"Why don't I give you half an hour?" Suzie stood before Niall could offer an argument. "Since arriving in Scotland, I've developed a taste for tablet. It's a bit like the condensed milk fudge we make at home. We call it Russian fudge. The sweet shop stocks it, so I'll grab some now. Oh, and I want a couple of postcards." She smiled sweetly at his brothers, but her eyes remained cool. "Thirty minutes."

Niall took a moment to admire the sway of her backside before she disappeared outside. His gaze raked his brothers. "Clock's ticking." He took petty pleasure in seeing Euan's mouth drop open.

"Aren't you gonna invite us to sit? Buy us a drink?" Colin demanded.

"No."

Colin blinked.

Niall picked up his beer. "Buy your own drinks."

Euan jerked his head at Colin, and he slunk toward the

bar. He returned with two pints of frothy ale.

Niall scrutinized his brothers. They had changed little, and their brawling had stamped their faces with scars. Their clothes bore dirt and wrinkles, suggesting they'd slept rough. Finally, when neither uttered a word, he said, "I thought you wanted to talk."

Euan and Colin exchanged an uneasy glance. Euan checked the men and women nearby, but no one was paying them attention. "We need money."

"No," Niall said without hesitation. He knew his brothers well. They'd keep pushing if he gave in to them, even a little. He doubted they'd changed. "How did you find me?"

"We've always known," Euan said.

Niall snorted. Until now, they hadn't thought him valuable. His mind went straight to his honey, and he wondered at their timing. "Is the rest of the family here?"

"Not yet," Euan said, his words a veiled threat.

"Why won't you give us money?" Colin asked. "We're family."

"When it suits you," Niall said. "I won't give you a penny, so I suggest you leave."

Euan and Colin exchanged another of those glances. Niall, who'd become excellent at reading body language, frowned. If he didn't know better, he'd assume someone or something had scared his brothers. And that didn't jibe with his memory of them.

"Was there anything else?" Niall prompted.

"Can we stay with you?" Euan asked.

"No," Niall said. "You made my life hell when I was

younger. You made me eat last, and I had to sleep on the floor. When I got a job, you stole my wages. Why would I give you anything now when I escaped that?"

"Family sticks together," Colin said.

Niall didn't rein in his snort of derision. "Really? That's the line you're gonna take with me now? I'll make this even clearer for you. I have worked for everything I own and continue to work to support myself. Unless you've changed radically, I doubt you have a job, which is why you want my money. How did you obtain the airfare from Canada?"

His brothers refused to meet his gaze, which tweaked his suspicions. He made a mental note to call a contact in Canada because knowledge was forearming. He wouldn't trust his brothers, no matter what assurances they gave. Experience had taught him well, ensuring no foolish repetition.

"Never mind," Niall said. "Listen well. You are not welcome in my home. You stole my childhood pocket money. It won't happen again."

"But we're your brothers. We were joking around," Colin said.

"I don't care what schemes you have going. Leave me out of them. You showed no concern for me as a cub, and nothing has changed." Niall spotted Suzie. "Goodbye."

His two brothers hovered, shock flashing over their faces before they went expressionless.

Colin took half a step closer. "But we're—"

Euan closed his meaty fist around Colin's forearm, stopping him from saying more. "Let's go. It's obvious

Runt thinks himself too good to associate with us now."
He whispered something to Colin that Niall didn't catch,
and Colin ceased his fight. He went willingly with Euan.
Niall watched them until they vanished out a side door,
every muscle in his body tense and ready for flight.

For a moment, his brothers' arrival had tossed him back
to his childhood, and the same feelings of inadequacy
and helplessness had filled him. Hatred and shame.
Determination to remove himself and not get sucked into
their lives.

Yeah, he'd felt like the *runt* again until Suzie had
squeezed his knee. The reassuring touch had righted him
and made him remember *Runt* had been past Niall. The
Niall he'd grown into was the man he wished to remain.

He had pride in his achievements and friends.

A mate.

His bear released a satisfied chuff, and Niall felt his lips
kick up at the corners. They were on the same page, with
Suzie their objective. Niall wasn't sure he could compete
against her goal to attend university, but she'd agree to stay
until his honey hit the stores. That was a win.

Suzie approached the table, several shopping bags in her
hands. "I purchased a sweater and some underwear. I need
more things, but I'll have to wait for a bigger shopping
center.

"You can come with me to Edinburgh next week when
I speak with the owners of a gym chain," Niall said. "I was
hoping they could help me test my product on the sly."

"Oh?" Suzie set her packages on the empty chair to her
right before she reclaimed her seat.

"Their gyms all have juice bars and serve healthy snacks. I wondered if they could use the honey as an ingredient in several of their products and observe the changes."

"How will you keep it secret?" Suzie asked.

"The gym owner was short of money and seeking a partner. I'm the partner who helped him. I prefer to approach him in person, but I'm positive he'll help."

"Sneaky," Suzie said. "It looks as if the kitchen is ready to open. Do you think we could order now? I'm starving."

"Did you check the menu?"

"I decided on fish and chips, although the steak and kidney pie sounded tempting."

"That's what I usually order. You can try some of mine."

Suzie's broad grin smoothed the last of his ruffled feathers, and he resolved not to think about his brothers until he and Suzie returned to the castle. He wanted to focus on this beautiful shifter and start the wooing process. He and his bear had a challenge before them, but that didn't daunt Niall because he thrived on challenges.

"Did you find your tablet?" he asked.

"I did. The sweet shop owner makes it herself, and she'd just put out a fresh batch. I bought enough to share. Do you have a sweet tooth?"

Niall huffed out a laugh. "I'm a bear. It goes with the territory."

"I'll need to use the gym every morning and perhaps start swimming again."

"Feel free to access the basement gym and heated pool anytime."

"Thanks."

Suzie's beam had him smiling in return. Heck, his mouth was hurting with all this uncharacteristic smiling. His bear huffed, amused, while Niall shook his head.

"Will your brothers cause trouble?"

That knocked the amusement out of him. "Yes, they can't help themselves. None of my brothers or sisters believe in hard work when taking the fruits of someone else's labors is much easier."

Suzie's expression held sympathy, and it warmed him inside. Apart from Cameron, no one had ever cared about him before. He'd had to fight and struggle to reach his current position.

"Do you think your brothers shot at us?"

"They didn't deny it," Niall said, tightening the grip on his beer. "They would've loudly protested their innocence but shrugged it off. It was as if I mentioned the sunny weather."

Suzie snorted. "Were they trying to scare us?"

Niall threw up his hands and almost sloshed beer over the table. "Who knows how their minds work? Maybe they wanted to frighten us. Me."

"They sounded desperate when they asked for money."

Niall tapped his free hand on the tabletop, his fingers striking one after the other in a rhythm. When he realized what he was doing, he stilled. Hell, he was regressing to old ways. Bad habits that let others know of his inner turmoil. But seeing his brothers again had plunked him right back to childhood memories and the uncaring cruelty they'd dealt him because he was unable to defend himself. He'd gone without food because he ate last and... Enough, dammit. He couldn't afford to let them into his head.

Niall considered Suzie's words. Yes, they'd almost pleaded toward the end. He recalled their love of gambling, and that made him wonder. "I need to set a private investigator on their tails. Someone to watch Euan and Colin, and another in Canada for the home front. I would do the job myself but prefer to focus on work."

"That makes sense. Do you have anyone in mind? Could we contact them now? My gut says you should move quickly and not worry about family disloyalty or anything stupid."

Niall grinned. "Thanks for the advice."

"Should I order our meals while you make your phone calls?"

Niall reached for his wallet and handed her two fifty-pound notes. "Order us another drink, too. The barman will remember my drink since I'm a regular."

When Suzie hustled off, Niall inhaled and pulled out his phone. The investigator who'd conducted the security clearances on the people who had offered to test his honey had done quick, efficient work. He'd contact him to tail Euan and Colin and ask him for recommendations for the overseas part of the assignment. He dialed and hung up after a productive conversation. Both tasks were underway, and Niall was confident of having the information he'd sought quickly.

Suzie sat, writing a postcard, and she glanced at him. "How did that go?"

"I can focus on my business and not worry about my brothers or family. And enjoy eating dinner with a beautiful woman."

"You flirt," she said, fluttering her eyelashes.

Niall laughed, his feel-good mood from earlier returning. Another first for him. In the past, he would've gone straight home and stewed about what mischief his brothers intended. The worry remained, yet it was manageable and less debilitating than before. Suzie was an excellent influence or maybe it was the fact she was his mate, and she had quickly become vital to him.

He'd noted the way Euan and Colin ogled her. They lacked respect for women and thought them suitable for only one thing. Niall knew better, and although he'd ensure that his brothers were never alone with Suzie, she'd be capable of taking them down. Physically, she was strong. She'd kept up with him and hadn't broken a sweat during their walk. She hadn't panicked when they'd faced danger.

His bear released another one of his chuffs, the sound full of the same satisfaction that flooded Niall. They'd chosen a strong woman who let nothing or no one intimidate her.

Now, they had to woo her and entice her into staying with them. Niall glanced at Suzie, ensnared her gaze, and winked. Let the games begin.

9

TOUCH ME...

SUZIE MELTED UNDER THE look in Niall's brown eyes, the heat and intense male interest followed by the amber glint of his bear shining through his irises. He sparked an interesting reaction in her. An unusual one that should've had her warning antenna blaring and her feline on high alert. She entered the castle's private rooms, supremely conscious of him at her side. Every part of her tingled, butterflies prickling in her stomach. Her clothes clung to her suddenly clammy skin, and she reached for him before the thought had solidified.

Sexual awareness.

She'd experienced this before but never at this intense level and never enough to tempt her.

It wasn't only her feline half pushing her, either.

She desired Niall despite his behavior when they'd first met. She'd taken a hard look at what she wanted.

Still music, but university wouldn't be the same without Edwina. Stepping out of routine for six months was exactly what she needed to recharge and regroup. After that, the decision to stay and work for Niall was easy.

He glanced at her when her fingers touched his forearm, and she froze like a rabbit sighting a leopard. Every emotion inside her slammed to a halt, and for a second, she forgot to breathe. Their gazes met and held, and she thought she spotted understanding flit across his features. Niall smiled, a natural curve of lips that lit him up. That smile made her feline purr, and Niall heard, dammit.

Without haste, he drew her closer and placed a soft kiss on her lips before setting her away. She stared at him, her heart beating so fast she wondered if he could hear it.

"How do you feel about a nightcap? Do you like Scottish whisky?"

Suzie wrinkled her nose, glad of the questions because all she needed to do was answer instead of struggling for a topic to break her rising tension. "Whisky and I don't get on together. I don't suppose you have a crème liqueur?"

Niall chuckled. "Take a seat while I organize drinks."

He led her into a small lounge with large picture windows overlooking the lake and gestured for her to take a seat. She dropped into a two-seater, but instead of savoring the gorgeous view of the tree-clad mountains and the still waters of the loch, she watched him, her heart still beating faster than normal.

She liked him a lot and craved more than a kiss. Much more.

Niall moved easily while he prepared their drinks, and

Suzie bit her lip. Normally, if she had met someone and admitted to lust, she'd be applying the mental handbrakes by now.

This wasn't happening with Niall.

Instead, she wanted to learn all the small details about him and more of what made him tick. Despite his grumpy demeanor, he'd fascinated her from the start, and tonight, she'd glimpsed the private man he didn't show to the rest of the world.

And... And she wanted to touch him and slide her body against his.

That notion gave her pause.

"Your drink," Niall said, handing her a crystal glass. "I added two ice cubes."

"Perfect," she said.

Instead of taking one of the chairs, Niall sat on the two-seater, his muscular thigh cozying up to her. Her hand trembled a fraction, setting the ice cubes tinkling.

If he asked, she would share a bed with him tonight.

And if not this evening, then soon.

That mental honesty had her taking a sip of the smooth drink, the faint bite of the liquid burning down her throat.

"A penny for your thoughts," Niall said.

Her gaze shot to his, and heat suffused her. Another tremor slipped through her body, yet she couldn't tear her focus off him. This was yearning. Desire.

"I...um..." She trailed off when he took the glass from her hands and set it aside with his.

He trailed the back of his fingers over her cheek, the physical contact arresting. "I'd like to kiss you again," he whispered. "Please."

Her head jerked in a faint nod, and he moved so fast she let out a startled *eep* as he set her on his knee.

"You don't mind, do you?" He stared into her eyes, a faint smile on his lips. "From the first moment I saw you..." He trailed off without finishing, but she understood.

Suzie got it.

He wanted her just as much as she wanted him. At that moment, Suzie surrendered the last of her restraint, and if anything, her feline purred louder.

Niall cupped her face and settled in to kiss her. Slow. Gentle and with a tenderness that had her toes curling. She pressed into him, enjoying the hardness of his muscles while his mouth sipped and savored hers, plucking nerve endings and sending sweet messages of arousal throughout her body.

She stared dazedly at him when he lifted his head.

"Should we move to the bedroom?" he asked, his husky voice showing that he, too, wasn't unaffected.

"Yes," she said without hesitation. "But you should know something first."

He stilled.

"Nothing bad," Suzie said. "But I haven't done this before."

"You're a virgin?" he asked, his voice turning hoarse.

"Yes."

"We should stop."

Suzie placed her hand on the open V of his shirt. His warm flesh seemed to brand her palm, but she left it in place, savoring the physical contact. "I want to be with you. I don't have a single doubt."

Niall grunted, a chuff that she thought was his inner bear. He cleared his throat. "I want you desperately, but we can wait."

"No! No," she repeated, the second time in a gentler tone. "My feline and I are on the same page. We have zero doubts."

"Are you on birth control?"

"Yes." She extended her arm, knowing that he would feel the faint bump of the implant London had insisted she, Edwina, and Anita have before they left for the gathering.

Niall gave a swift nod and lifted her into his arms. He strode rapidly through the castle until he reached a closed door. In seconds, he had it open, and they were inside a large chamber with an elegant and ginormous four-poster bed. Niall shouldered the door closed before stalking to the bed and setting her on the soft mattress.

Suzie watched him while he toed off his shoes and joined her on the bed. Not once did her inner self shriek or demand to know what she thought she was doing. That told her everything. Suzie reached for Niall, thrilling at his weight as he leaned over to kiss her again. Once again, he started slowly. He kissed the hollow of her throat and the valley between her breasts before he settled to kiss her mouth. This time, the kisses were deep and drugging. Intoxicating. They left her breathless and gripping his shoulders as an anchor. As he kissed her, buttons loosened, and clothing landed on the floor beside the bed. He paused to slip off her sandals and removed her shorts until all she wore was her bra and panties.

Suzie glanced down her almost naked body at her mismatched bra and panties. *Should've done the laundry.* "Aren't you taking off your clothes?"

"Not now," he said, his fingers trailing across the swell of one breast. "Since you haven't done this before, I want to ensure you enjoy every second. Concentrate on you and your pleasure. Mine can come later."

Wow. The couple of boyfriends who'd tried to take things further than she'd wanted hadn't considered her wants or needs at all.

Uncertainty drifted through her. Not about giving herself to Niall but the practicalities of sex. "What should I do?"

"All you need to do," Niall said, "is tell me if you're not enjoying how I'm touching you. That's your job."

"I can do that."

He smiled with encouragement and stole another kiss that drove every thought and worry from her mind. Niall trailed kisses down her neck and paused at the mating site at the base of her neck, laving the spot with his rough tongue. Suzie trembled, arousal darting to all corners of her body. She clasped her shoulders and wriggled against him. When he lifted his head, his brown eyes had turned golden, and his chest heaved.

"I cannot wait to taste you, sweet lass." He turned her a fraction and unhooked her bra.

She tensed a fraction until she witnessed the awe in his expression as he removed the lacey garment. He lowered his head to kiss the curve of one breast while his fingers cupped the weight of her other. The twin sensations tore through her, the soft, tormenting stroke of his fingers and the dampness of his mouth leaving an empty ache at the juncture of her thighs.

She plunged her fingers into his hair, holding him close and sighing when he took one nipple into his warm mouth. He drew on the bud, and she sighed as he bathed the puckered crest with his tongue.

"More," she demanded.

"Your wish is my command."

Niall played with her breasts, kissing and sucking and now and then pinching. The jolt of pain was surprising, but it left her body humming with delight, and she bucked against him, needing more. He stroked and caressed her ribs and hips before slowly moving down her body. Her breathing turned harsh while her muscles tensed.

"I can stop," he reminded her.

"No! No, don't stop. Please."

To her relief, he didn't halt. Instead, he whisked off her panties and stroked the tense muscles of her thighs until she relaxed. He parted her legs, leaning close and kissing her where seconds ago he'd stroked. Niall moved his attentions closer to the heart of her, and her pulse kicked up another notch. He brushed his fingers along delicate nether lips, then followed a similar path with his tongue.

Sensations writhed through her instantly, and she cried out, not knowing whether to be pleased or embarrassed at her body's quick reaction to his touch.

"Aw, lass. You taste sweet as the finest honey." He hummed as he swept his tongue along her slit and petted her clit.

Suzie groaned, lost in the instant pleasure, but to her disappointment, he backed off the direct stimulation. Instead, he slipped one finger inside her, massaging her internally.

She lifted into the sensual stroke, trying not to worry about how wet she'd become. Niall added another finger, but this time, he teased her clit with his tongue, and the delicious assault had a shudder racing through her. His fingers hit a spot inside her, and she cried out. The stroke of his fingers and the sweep of his tongue lit a flashfire within her. For a second, she hovered at a point she could only describe as a combination of pleasure and pain, then those talented fingers of his rubbed again, and the sensations crescendoed. Her body convulsed in an explosion of blissful delight. She shuddered while fire swarmed over her skin, and Niall whispered sweet nothings.

Gradually, she came back to herself and glanced down to meet his golden gaze.

"Okay?"

"Very okay," she whispered.

"Are you ready for more?"

"So ready," she replied.

Niall sat up and stripped off his shirt to reveal his muscular chest and the light dusting of hair. He stood and removed his shorts and underwear, standing back to let her look her fill. He was large all over. *All over.*

His cock...

"Don't worry, lass. We'll fit together perfectly. I

promise." It was easy to hear the amusement in his voice.

"If you say so," she said.

He laughed, the sound full of mirth as he slid back onto the bed and drew her into his arms.

"What should I do?"

"Touch me," he said, so she did.

"Ah, maybe not there, lass," he said abruptly.

Suzie glanced up and met his rueful grin.

"You test my control."

"And that's a bad thing?"

"It is right now when I want to make your first time memorable," he said and placed her hands on his shoulders. "You can touch later. I promise."

He kissed her again, sipping at her lips before he made a deep sound in his throat. Suddenly the sweet kiss was full of hunger, full of heat. Suzie's breath caught, and she arched against his chest, wanting to be as close as possible. She'd thought she might feel a flicker of fear or at least anxiety, but every one of his kisses, his touches, made her body hum and her pulse race. Her feline purred, pleased with this turn of events, and that told her everything.

The wet pull of his mouth at her breast had her paying closer attention and savoring every instinctive reaction of her body. She ran her fingers over his back, the hitch in his breathing taking her by surprise. Suzie tested his muscles, squeezing bulging biceps and triceps and enjoying his soft groan and the way they contracted. It made her realize that she held power, too, and the ability to turn him inside out.

Mine, she thought and wriggled beneath his bulk, drawing another groan from him.

"I wanted to go slow," he said.

"Not necessary." And that was true because she ached for more. She'd had a taster earlier, and now she wanted to experience everything. "Niall."

His sharp intake of breath told her he understood, and he parted her legs with one of his muscular thighs.

"Are you certain?"

"Not a single doubt," she replied.

"Thank the stars," he muttered fervently.

He kissed her again, another of those sweet kisses that turned her inside out. At the same time, he guided his cock and pushed slowly into her.

It hurt, a shaft of pain that took her by surprise even though she'd known she might experience discomfort. She winced, and Niall stilled immediately.

He brushed a lock of hair off her cheek, his brown eyes somber. "It will get better, lass."

She nodded and reached up to kiss him because he looked stricken, his features drawn tight. The pain had receded, and now she merely felt pressure and fullness, allowing her to relax slightly.

"Okay?" At her nod, Niall drew back a fraction and slid deeper. This stroke was smooth and didn't bother her in the slightest. With each successive thrust, her grip on his shoulders lessened, the twists of enjoyable sensations offsetting the previous shock of pain.

Niall paused to smile down at her. "Better?"

"Please move." The words were so rapid that they ran together.

Niall kissed the tip of her nose before taking her mouth

with hunger. He slipped his hands beneath her bottom and changed the angle of his drives into her. Suzie clung to him, overcome by the emotions and the pleasure that roared through her now. This... The intimacy was so much more than she'd imagined.

Each time he filled her, he connected with a sensitive spot deep inside her, and when he caressed her clit, a ferocious heat burst through her, taking her body by storm. The walls of her sex pulsated, and Niall groaned. His face twisted with a primitive hunger that pushed her pulse into fast and choppy. His bear was clearly visible in his eyes, and Suzie released a low growl—her feline exerting control. Niall's nostrils flared, and he increased the pace of his strokes. He ceased his thrusts abruptly, his shaft buried deep inside her.

"Suzie," he whispered.

In answer, she wrapped her arms around his shoulders and sought his kiss. *Wow!* The wait had been worth it. So worth it.

Niall pulled free of her and rearranged their bodies. His warm arms enfolded her against his chest as he cuddled her for long moments.

When he finally pulled away, she protested.

"Shush, lass. I'll be back in a moment." Niall stood and padded into the en suite. The water turned on, and he returned a few minutes later carrying a damp cloth.

"What—?"

"You'll be sore," he said in a matter-of-fact voice. "This will help."

The cloth was warm against her flesh and soothing.

"There you go," he said, standing again. He disappeared into the en suite and returned to bed.

"Now what?" Suzie said, feeling a little awkward and unsure. What was the protocol? Did she return to her bed?

His brown eyes twinkled as he slid into the bed beside her and tugged her against him. "Now, we cuddle, sleep a little, and depending on how you feel, we enjoy ourselves again."

"Oh." Suzie relaxed and pressed her cheek against his brawny chest. "That sounds lovely."

"It does," he agreed, and a rumble slipped past his lips.

It sounded as if his bear agreed with the plan. Suzie smiled and let her eyes flutter closed. Best day ever.

10

BEARS IN THE WOODS

S UZIE GRINNED AS SHE raced into her bedroom, dressed in Niall's robe and carrying the clothes she'd worn yesterday. A glance from her tower window showed sunshine, and after a leisurely shower, she opted for shorts and a T-shirt. A walk before breakfast to enjoy the fine weather, she decided, before she headed to the office to work with Niall. It was the working bit that surprised her a little. She liked the gruff bear very much, and now that he'd told her about his past, she understood his determination to succeed and his attitude toward his family. Her younger siblings sometimes drove her nuts, but she loved them and would do anything for the pests, as she called them. Her parents, too. They'd been strict with her but fair, and they had her respect.

Niall hadn't mentioned his parents, but they must've known what was going on with their children. Shaking her head, she arranged her hair in a haphazard ponytail. She thrust her feet into sandals and headed out to explore the gardens Niall kept for his private use.

Outside, she inhaled the crisp air tinted with pine and roses. The nearby flower bed was awash with yellow roses, and a gardener was busy removing the dead flowers. He dipped his head in a respectful nod.

"Good morning," Suzie said. "Which is the best way to walk?"

"The master usually wanders through the flower beds and into the forest. There's a trail that joins the one that circles the lake. It will take you about an hour."

"Thank you. That sounds perfect." Suzie waved goodbye and strolled between the flower beds, directing her steps to the path the gardener had shown her.

After the bright morning sun, the shade under the trees was welcome. The pine needles muted her footsteps, which allowed her to spot shy forest creatures. A red squirrel darted along the branches of an oak tree and jumped to the next—a beech of some kind. The animal chittered at her as if scolding her for interrupting its foraging, then flitted away with a flick of its bushy tail.

The crack of a branch had her freezing, and she peered through the trees. A flash of color enlightened her. A deer. It darted away with more crashing, and silence fell again, broken only by a singing bird. The path sloped upward, giving her views of the castle and the lake, and she halted to take photos before glancing at her watch.

Oops! She'd need to hustle if she wanted breakfast before she started work.

Angus served traditional Scottish breakfasts with bacon, square sausage, beans, fried eggs, and tattie scones. Sometimes, the breakfast included link sausages or slices of haggis and grilled tomatoes. She was a devotee.

Suzie jogged along the forest path and down the hill to the lakeshore. Halfway down, a musky scent reached her. Not unusual because the shifters attending the gathering had access to this area of the estate, but something—an inner instinct—had her steps slowing and her feline surfacing. She warily scanned the shadows beneath the tall oaks, beech trees, and the lower leafy bushes full of lush summer growth.

When she saw nothing, and the birds continued to sing overhead, she shook herself and hustled down the path to the lake. The scent bothered her, but Suzie pushed onward, each of her senses ultra-aware and processing information at top speed. She'd reached the lake's edge when a bear padded from behind a bramble patch. Suzie's heart jumped before she forced herself to keep moving. Scotland didn't have native wild bears—not any longer. This was a shifter and a male, judging by his size. His shaggy coat was a rich brown, and he scrutinized her intently.

Suzie stared back, instinctively refusing to let the shifter intimidate her. A large contingent of bears had attended the gathering. She'd met a few but didn't recognize this one despite his familiar scent.

The bear retreated, padding out of sight as quickly as he'd appeared.

Suzie waited for the count of ten before breaking into a

jog to avoid being too late. She rushed into the breakfast room, breathless and warm from her hustle. Niall had already started with a heaped plate of sausage, eggs, bacon, and other delicious items when she slid into the seat opposite him.

"Sorry, I'm late. It was such a lovely morning. I went for a walk. The loop around the lake took me longer than I planned."

His brows cocked, his silence full of questions.

"Okay, I admit it. I dallied watching the red squirrels. They are so cute."

"See anyone else?"

"I saw a bear shifter, but we didn't speak. He remained in his bear form."

"He?"

"Yeah, the bear was freakin' huge." She cast him a glance. "How big are you in your bear form?"

Niall choked out a laugh, and she rolled her eyes.

"Mind out of the gutter, Sinclair. Typically, bear shifters are large, and this one was immense."

Angus arrived carrying a loaded plate, and Suzie eyed it with pleasure. "Thank you, Angus. That looks delicious." She reached for toast and buttered it before digging into the bacon, eggs, and square sausage she'd become enamored with since first tasting the meat.

"Tea or coffee?" Angus inquired.

"Tea, please. English Breakfast."

Angus retreated, returning a few minutes later with a large teapot. He poured tea for them, remembering her preferences without asking. She gave a happy sigh before she took a bite of toast. Adapting to this life would be easy, but she'd gain weight without exercise.

"What are we doing today?" she asked.

"I thought we'd review the designs for the honey labels and the packaging. My friend also sent me a package of user questionnaires. We need to review them and compile the information in a usable form."

"I can review the surveys for you. I'll create a spreadsheet. How many are there?"

"Around a hundred," Niall said as his phone rang. "Sinclair."

It was the local investigator, and Suzie heard every word of his report. He'd tracked Niall's brothers to a cottage at the edge of the village. His gut told him they weren't staying there legally since he'd contacted the owner, who was visiting relatives in Australia and had left the property empty. He'd spotted one brother entering but hadn't seen both siblings. He intended to watch the premises and follow them if the brothers left together.

"Thank you," Niall said. "Please send me daily reports, and if they do anything suspicious, call me immediately."

"Will do." The terse male ended the call.

"A man of few words."

"Yes," Niall said. "I like working with him because he doesn't mess around."

Once they reached Niall's office, Suzie took a pile of surveys and began analyzing them, transferring the questionnaires to a spreadsheet for easier comparison. The job was fascinating, and the hours flew. It surprised her when Angus arrived with a lunch tray.

"Is it that time already?" she asked, blinking at the clock near Niall's desk. Her gaze slid back to the surveys. Only three more to go. "I might finish inputting the info from the last three questionnaires, then I can print out the results while we're eating." *Huh!* Where was Niall? She hadn't even heard him leave.

"The food won't spoil," Angus assured her, his manner gruff. It was an improvement from his usual clipped replies, and she sensed the approval beneath his words. It made her curious, and she wondered how Niall had inspired such loyalty from the older man.

Pushing aside her curiosity, she resumed work. Half an hour later, she stood and stretched. During that time, Niall had reappeared, and she discovered him eyeing her with interest.

"What?"

Niall broke into a boyish grin, and her heartbeat blipped.

"I enjoy watching you. Let's eat, then walk for fresh air and sunshine. We can review your spreadsheet info once we return."

They demolished the food, and once they wandered outside into the rose garden, Niall took her hand.

"Thank you for your hard work this morning."

"I enjoyed it," Suzie said, and it was the truth. Organizing the information had been easy enough, and she liked using her secretarial skills.

"Tell me about your music. What type of course do you prefer? And how can I help?" Niall guided her on the same walking track she'd taken during the morning. "We'll see if this enormous bear is still hiding in the woods."

Suzie huffed, and he laughed. Something he didn't do often, but it suited him. She stopped walking, and when he looked askance at her, she stood on tiptoes to kiss him. Niall hummed his approval and drew her closer, arms wrapping her in an embrace. Their kiss deepened until he was all that existed in her world, along with his enticing honey scent. When they pulled apart, they were both breathing hard.

"What was that for?"

"I like you," she whispered, going for truth.

"Our thoughts align," he said in a rough voice. He released her but held her hand as they walked into the shade of two towering beech trees. They ambled in silence, but it was comfortable.

Suzie tugged him to a halt when she spied a red squirrel, and she leaned against him while they watched the tiny creature's antics. The path dipped when they headed toward the lake, and belatedly, Suzie realized the forest had gone silent. Not a bird chirped, and the squirrels had disappeared from the treetops.

Niall's hand tightened on hers, and her steps slowed. She turned to him, about to speak when he tensed. His gaze was on where she'd seen the bear this morning, except now two bears sat watching them.

"Niall?" she asked in an undertone.

He sighed, a harsh sound containing irritation. "My brothers."

"But this is private property. How did they get past the fence?"

"Nothing much will stop a determined trespasser," Niall said, maintaining his watchful air.

Movement from behind them had Suzie shifting her stance, and what she saw alarmed her.

"Niall," she said, tugging at his sleeve.

"I see them. Shift and run for help. Speak with Angus. He'll know what to do."

"I can't leave you here alone," Suzie protested. Two men appeared from the trees, causing her stomach to drop. They weren't close enough for her to scent them, so she wasn't certain if they were shifters. But two bears and four men against one. Niall wouldn't have a chance.

"Please," Niall repeated in an undertone. "I can't fight if you're in danger."

Despite the circumstances, everything inside her went soft. "All right but fight dirty. Strike first and take them by surprise. They're big but soft around the middle. I bet they rely on their size to intimidate, but they're not great in hand-to-hand combat."

Suzie subtly distanced herself and broke into a run. The men let her go, and she increased her speed, tearing toward the castle for help.

Niall breathed easier once Suzie disappeared into the trees surrounding the lake, and none of the men tried to stop or follow her. Once he lost sight of her, he turned his attention back to his brothers. He'd known they were trouble but betraying him this way cut like a knife. His parents had always drilled into him and his siblings about family first. He sneered at Euan before he let his gaze slide to Colin, both still in their bear forms. Their urgent need for money had overcome their principles.

"What do you truly want?" Niall demanded. *Strike first. Learn what they expected from him.*

"Boss wants to speak with you," one of the hulking brutes said.

That was an apt description, and Suzie was right. They appeared soft around the middle. He wondered what his brothers were doing with humans. He didn't recognize them but committed their faces to memory. They were all bald or with shaven heads, tall, and wearing uniform-like dark clothes.

"Why? I don't know your boss."

The man standing to his left was older and kept his distance. A sense of familiarity jostled at the back of his brain. He'd seen this man before but couldn't recall where.

The men exchanged grins. No, they were more leers.

"Your lady is sexy. She a good lay?" the man asked, waggling his black brows.

"Who?" Niall played dumb and batted down anger and his bear. *Not the right time.*

"The one we let leave. The one we saw you kissing," the man said, his smirk in evidence again. "She knows."

Niall cursed, every muscle tensing. Suzie was part of this?

"You coming with us peaceful like, or do we have to jump you?"

"I'm a busy man. Tell your boss to make an appointment like everyone else," Niall said.

"He's busy too," the man said.

The men sniggered, but Niall didn't shift his attention from the speaker. It must be related to his honey. It was the only thing that made sense.

"You tell your boss he can produce his own honey. I have no intention of letting him steal my formula."

The big man shrugged, and he grinned. "Why should he when you do his work? He has your honey, but a few crucial parts are missing."

"You broke into my research station," Niall snarled, taking half a step forward.

The man straightened, and the others closed around him, not appearing as casual now.

"Stop mucking around," the man said. "You're coming with us. Why not make it easy on yourself?"

Niall darted forward, smashing his weight against the nearest man. He went down with a yelp. Niall punched hard and used his size and fitness to knock two more men over before the rest grabbed him. Someone hit him from behind, and everything turned black.

11

TROUBLE AND DISAPPOINTMENT

"ANGUS!" SUZIE BURST INTO Niall's private apartments and hoped the steward was nearby. Thankfully, he appeared from the salon before she filled her lungs to bellow again. What would they do to Niall? She should've stayed, shouldn't have listened to him. Suzie could've helped. Their assailants might've outnumbered them, but Isabella had taught her to protect herself.

"What is it, Miss Suzie?" Angus appeared alert, his composure unruffled.

She probably looked like something the cat dragged in—a house cat, that is. She drew a sharp breath and another to steady herself. "It's Niall. We walked around the lake, and men accosted us. Niall told me to come for help."

Angus didn't muck around. He barked several orders into his phone before bustling to the rear of the castle and the garden where she and Niall had first walked. She found four burly gardeners awaiting Angus's instructions.

"Can you show us where you were?" Angus asked.

She was still gasping but nodded and set off at a trot. It took about ten minutes to reach the area where the men had intercepted them. The bellows of an enraged bear met them, and Suzie slowed, uncertain of what she'd find. Angus and his men didn't hesitate and rushed past. Swallowing her trepidation, Suzie followed more slowly. Upon rounding the last corner, she immediately noticed a massive bear. He lurched toward two smaller bears. As she watched, spellbound, one bear fled. The massive bear paused, which allowed the second bear to retreat. The men with them had vanished.

"It doesn't appear Mr. Niall required our help," Angus said.

Suzie thought that was a grin twitching his firm lips, but she couldn't be sure.

"Did any of them get away?" Angus directed his question at the bear.

The bear shook his head before focusing on Suzie. His snarl held a nasty edge, and she took an involuntary step back, her heart suddenly racing.

Angus shot her a concerned glance and casually stepped between them. The bear—Niall—released a sharp chuff that might've been humor, but given the display of sharp white teeth, Suzie thought otherwise. What the hell? He'd held her hand earlier. Kissed her. What had happened during her absence?

What had the men done? Said?

"Go home," Angus said. "I'll pick up your clothes, and the men and I will check for other trespassers."

Niall didn't reply but swung his big body around and broke into a lope.

Angus sent her a long look.

"What? I did nothing except run for help. I have no idea of those men's identities. The two bears are Niall's brothers. They ambushed us when we had dinner last night at the pub. I know their names, but that's all."

"Something has upset Niall. He seldom shifts to his bear," Angus said. "You'd better stay with me until we can work this out."

"Joy," Suzie muttered, not trying to hide her annoyance. "No matter what I do with Niall, I can't win."

Niall raced up the hill and into the trees before his steps slowed. The knot on the back of his head ached, but worse, his mate had betrayed him.

"Mine. Mine. Mine."

His bear refused to listen, and now that he was in bear form, he simply fumed while his beast shifted his thoughts to berries. Sighing, Niall released the illusion of control and allowed his bear to wander and explore as he hadn't in months.

They stumbled on a familiar scent that had a growl rising. *His traitorous brothers.* Huh! They'd think twice before they considered him too weak to defend himself. He'd woken rapidly after the blow to his head and shown them, but it had surprised even him when his bear was so much bigger than them. It had been fear glinting in their eyes before they'd run off. If they'd had a tail, it would've tucked between their legs. Yeah, he'd inflicted several blows they'd had no defense against, and satisfaction slid through him at this. His bear had shown them not to treat him like the weakest. He was no longer the runt.

Niall followed the trail to where it ended at the six-foot-tall stone wall surrounding his land. He'd electrify the wall or place shards of glass atop the fence. His brothers should reconsider trespassing again.

Niall continued tracking and discovered a section of the wall had crumbled, allowing the human portion of the attack team to cross into his land. He planned to repair it and have men patrol the wall until things settled. His brothers needed to go home, and he'd happily escort them to the plane.

He wasn't sure of their motives, but they were involved in something murky and determined to drag him with them. They had said little, allowing one human to do the talking. The head man must have had shifter blood or a connection to their world. Otherwise, Euan and Colin wouldn't work with him. He'd contact the PI once he arrived home.

Then there was Suzie.

He averted his thoughts from the double-dealing woman and firmly instructed his bear to return home to the castle. No, he'd ask her about what the men had said before he jumped to conclusions. That was the right thing to do.

His bear got distracted several times, and they discovered a wild bee colony near the edge of a sunny clearing. It made his heart sing since there weren't many hives of this nature around. He observed bees feeding on heather across the valley. Heather honey. *Yum.* His favorite.

Home, he told his bear.

His bear lifted his nose and inhaled before chuffing and taking off at a lope. *Suzie.* It seemed their confrontation would happen sooner rather than later.

Suzie headed straight for her room, stripped, and jumped in the shower. Not only was she covered in dust and dirt, but she smelled disgustingly sweaty. Her stink offended her, and she desperately needed to replace it with lavender and oranges.

Once out of the shower, she donned a short denim skirt and a navy blue blouse showcasing her breasts. She tied back her hair into a stubby ponytail and thrust her feet into sandals. Then she searched for Niall, wanting to learn what she'd done now.

She had a clear conscience, and after those men had pushed her around, she was in the mood for a fight—bear or not.

Suzie found him in the office, his hair damp from a shower. Sensing her presence, he lifted his head and glared at her. The chair creaked under his weight.

Suzie plonked a hand on her right hip and gave him attitude. "What have I supposedly done now?"

"You worked with those humans and told them the best place to find us. They have heard rumors about my honey and want it."

"Why didn't you kick me out of the castle instead of letting me have a shower?" If she'd been in her feline form, the hair along her spine would've stood to attention. This fool bear didn't get it. Her parents had raised her to value honor and integrity. Loyalty. While she'd bucked against authority and being told what to do, the other lessons had stuck. She understood the need for secrecy with Niall's project and would never share proprietary information. Then there was the friendship aspect. She'd considered him a friend, and one didn't rat on their buddies. That was high on her list of most important rules.

"Angus is clearing your room now."

Her brows rose, and her fingernails dug into her palms. She worked hard to keep her temper in check because nothing annoyed her more than someone questioning her honesty.

"You didn't think to speak with me first? I've done nothing wrong."

"I found you wandering my home. That's when I first met you."

She rolled her eyes. "Let it go, will you? I was wrong, but I've been too busy working to meet other people. When have I been alone?"

"You went for a walk by yourself this morning." The

silky words slid past the barriers she'd placed around her smoldering temper.

"I saw a bear when I was walking. I told you that. Why would I tell you if I were selling you out? Think, Niall. Use that big brain of yours. Whoever told you I'm a traitor was trying to push you off balance and make you doubt yourself. Hell, lock me up again if you don't believe me. The only men I recognized were your brothers, and I met them once at the pub. I haven't spoken to them since."

"So you say."

Suzie threw up her hands. "I haven't had time to call them even if I knew their phone numbers. Last night, we were together until I went to my room and retired for the night. I took a quick walk this morning because it was such a nice day, and you had phone calls to make. Niall, I believe in you and your product and want you to succeed."

"People have told me that before. I believed them, and it was my worst decision ever."

"Fine," Suzie snapped. "I'll return to the gathering and go home afterward. And although my word doesn't mean a thing to you, I won't discuss you or your honey with anyone." Suzie whirled and marched to the door, so disappointed with Niall that tears gathered in her eyes. Why would he believe some stranger over her? Suzie resisted the urge to slam the door, closing it softly instead.

She held back her tears until she reached the bedroom she'd used since working with Niall. She found Angus inside with her belongings packed into her bag. He sent her a sympathetic glance, his thin shoulders hunching momentarily. Suzie swiped the back of her hand over her eyes and sniffed.

"Can I return to my old room and stay until the gathering ends?"

He surveyed her with none of the coolness she'd received from him in the past. Angus gave a faint nod. "They're about to serve afternoon tea. Why don't you find your friends? Have tea with them, and by the time you're finished, I'll have your belongings in your room for you."

Suzie nodded. "Which way should I enter the public part of the castle? I don't want Niall to accuse me of trespassing again."

"This way, Miss Suzie," Angus said, his voice softer than usual.

He showed her to an oak door and directed her down a short flight of stairs. When she reached the bottom, she recognized her location. This was the doorway she'd gone through to get to Niall's private part of the castle. The same sign—*private: no entry beyond this point* barred her way. She stepped over it, and when she turned to say thank you, Angus had already vanished. Suzie sighed. And here she thought they were becoming friends.

She didn't feel like company or the inevitable questions Scott and Liam would ask if she found them. Instead, she retraced her steps to her old room. Angus was efficient, and her suitcase sat beside the bed. Her handbag rested on the bedcovers, and she plucked up the black leather strap and draped it over her shoulder. She'd walk to the village and purchase stamps for her postcards. If she posted them this week, they'd arrive home before her. Also, she'd get more tablet. The sweet fudge-like squares were addictive. Too bad if they were fattening. Currently, her thoughts were consumed by Niall's stubbornness, with no concern for anything else.

She stomped down the castle driveway and through the side gate, acknowledging the guard with a glower. Guilt rose in her when he sent her a respectful nod. She sighed and dropped the attitude.

"Thank you," she said to the guard and continued walking, her pace slower now that the distance between her and Niall had increased. She liked him and had never experienced such ease with another man. She admired his drive and determination. What she didn't like was the fact she'd given her virginity to her mate, and he'd been as eager as her. Their night together had been better than she'd ever imagined, and now he was accusing her of traitorous acts.

She would never backstab him.

Suzie drew a deep breath, attempting to settle her anger into something productive. His brothers were a sore point with Niall, and from the little she'd learned, she could understand he'd feel betrayed if she'd joined forces with them to take him down. They clearly desired Niall's life in Scotland. His money and position. Euan hadn't hidden his avarice.

How had they known Niall was here? Niall had told her he'd left home and hadn't seen anyone in his family since they hadn't cared. But what if they'd kept tabs on him and known his location all the time? What if they had waited for the perfect opportunity to use Niall?

Greed was an easy motive, but what if revenge had played a part?

Niall sounded surprised that his brothers had enough money to purchase a plane ticket. Her brow furrowed in deep concentration. Immediately, her mother's words zapped into her mind, and she smoothed her forehead. No premature lines for her, thank you very much.

Once she entered the village proper, she slowed, her gaze lingering on the storefronts. She stopped at one with a display of scarves. A stack of tartan rugs was visible through the window. Her sisters would love a scarf, and it wouldn't be too weighty in her luggage. Suzie opened the door and smiled at the bell's tinkle announcing her presence. It rang in the tune of Scotland the Brave. She spied a rack of tartan skirts. Her eyes widened as her gaze lit on the label. It was a sign—Paisley tartan.

Size was easy enough since she and her mother could be twins. It was a matter of seconds to find the perfect one. She chose scarves for her two younger sisters, which meant she only required something for her father and younger brother. A paisley tie. Perfect. That would please her mother. She'd add a gift box of tablet since she'd acquired her sweet tooth from her father. He'd enjoy the sugary treat. Her younger brother would turn up his nose at clothes, but he loved puzzles. Wow! She should've visited this store before. All her shopping completed in one hit. She'd have to tell Liam and Scott since they needed gifts for their families.

With her purchases paid for, she hit the post office for stamps before deciding to have a coffee and plan her next steps.

Niall.

Her mind kept returning to the stubborn bear like a homing pigeon. His lack of trust hurt, and once she proved her innocence, she intended to make him pay. Her brow did that crinkle thing again. She felt it and chided herself even as she smoothed away her frown. He could take her sightseeing in Edinburgh and for a swanky afternoon tea with a glass of bubbles.

Suzie chose the next cafe and walked inside. She settled her parcels on an empty seat and sat at a table by the rear window overlooking a park with dozens of children playing.

A plan.

Despite her bravado, her shoulders drooped because she had no idea what to do next. Niall had coldly kicked her out of his life, his expression resembling a marble statue. There was no trace of the passionate and jovial man from the previous night. He'd treated her callously, as if she'd been a business transaction he wanted completed, then tossed aside.

A shiver ran through her, and those wretched tears flooded her eyes again. She blinked hard, and none too soon because the waitress arrived to take her order.

"I'll have a pot of tea and a scone with jam and cream, please." Suzie tacked on a smile and thought she managed a creditable job.

"Yes, miss." The young woman hustled away, her crisp white apron rustling.

Ten minutes later, when she felt more fortified and relaxed, she paid more attention to her surroundings. Two men dressed in black sat at a table in the cafe while other customers hurriedly departed. They cast anxious glances over their shoulders, and two mothers called their children to them, their voices hoarse with alarm.

The waitress reluctantly approached the men, her steps slow and hesitant. Suzie stiffened and carefully dragged in a lungful of air to test their scent. Human and badly in need of a shower. Those leather jackets were warm for a summer day, even one in Scotland.

"H-hello," the waitress said, and her hand holding her order pad visibly trembled.

"H-hello," one man mocked.

The second man laughed, the end of his mirth sounding more like a giggle.

Suzie scowled at the bullies.

"C-can I take your o-order?" The girl tried hard not to stutter, but she was flustered.

Suzie stood and crossed the short distance to the girl. She patted her on the shoulder and took the order pad from her. "I'll take their order. You serve the other customers."

The waitress stared blankly at her since they could both see the café had magically emptied. "Thanks," she whispered after Suzie gave her an encouraging nod.

Suzie focused on the men. Now that she was closer, she could see they had ink on their chests and arms. Gang members of some description, given the patch on their jackets. Both had pale complexions and black hair, with one displaying signs of excessive drinking. The other had a bulbous nose and a cracked front tooth.

She smiled when she'd rather rip them a new one for tormenting a young girl trying to do her job. "Can I take your order, please?"

"We w-want the o-other girl," Ruddy Cheeks said.

"She's busy right now," Suzie said, pencil poised. "I'm helping. Now, what can I get you?"

"We want our usual morning tea," Bulbous Nose snapped. "One of everything and tea."

Ah! Now Suzie understood. This was a shakedown racket. "Of course. That will be expensive, so I'll need your credit card."

"We don't pay," Ruddy Cheeks said with a growl.

"Then you won't be getting any food," Suzie supplied sweetly.

"Who's stopping us from taking it, girlie?" Bulbous Nose snapped.

"Me," Suzie said.

12

I HATE BULLIES

S UZIE STARED AT THE two men. They were not
attractive specimens. Along with having an aversion
to water and soap, their clothes reeked of cigarette smoke,
and Bulbous Nose's faded black T-shirt bore a red splotch
that brought blood to mind.

She pulled out her phone and hit several buttons.

"Who're ya ringing?" Ruddy Cheeks demanded.

"The cops. This is extortion, and it's against the law."

"Ya bluffin'," Ruddy Cheeks snarled.

"Try me." She held up a hand as if to stop him talking.
"Yes. This is Suzie from the Full Cup Tea shop. I have
two male customers causing a disturbance. Could I have
assistance in evicting them, please? Five minutes? That's
fine." Suzie hung up and eyed the two men expectantly. If
anything, they appeared nonplussed.

"You're shittin' us," Ruddy Cheeks said finally.

"Nope," Suzie chirped. "You're bullies and rely on scaring people and forcing them to do your bidding. I don't care how big and bad you are. I'm cranky, and you came across me at the wrong time."

"Them's fightin' words," Bulbous Nose said. "And you a tiny thing against two men."

"Wow," Suzie said, amazed one man could be so stupid. She had confidence since she'd trained with Isabella. Then, there was her shifter status, which made her stronger and faster than humans.

Evidently, Ruddy Cheeks wasn't as foolish as Bulbous Nose. He rose and pushed back his chair. It scraped across the tiles while he glowered at her.

Suzie stood her ground, watchful and cautious. One of these idiots was going to break and hit her, and she hoped her confidence wasn't misplaced.

It was Bulbous Nose who made the first move. He jumped up and sprang at her. Suzie moved automatically, the endless drills Isabella had subjected her to now instinct. She stuck out her foot, and Bulbous Nose sprawled headfirst into the neighboring table. Empty plates and a half-eaten sausage roll went flying on impact. Cups and saucers crashed to the floor, and one thumped Bulbous Nose over the head. Cold tea dripped over him, and he cursed, something inventive that made Suzie's brows rise. She hadn't heard that one before. She grinned, taking mental notes. One never knew when an excellent mouth-rounding oath would come in handy.

Bulbous Nose climbed to his feet and charged. Suzie used her speed to dodge him, then seized him from behind.

She applied her foot to the back of his knee, and he went down. Unfortunately, Ruddy Cheeks had come to his senses and shoved her away from his friend.

"Leave my brother alone," he shouted.

She was lucky these two used their size and appearance to intimidate people, yet at heart, they were cowards. When someone stood up to them, they folded under the pressure.

"If you leave, I'll call off the cops," she said sweetly.

The front doorbell tinkled, snapping them out of their standoff. An older woman stalked inside and summed up the situation with one glance. She set her shopping bags on the counter, her lined face full of contempt. She wore a tweed skirt with a faint dusting of flour on the hem while her salt and pepper hair was tied back in a braid. The wisps that had escaped softened the woman's lined face.

"Georgia!"

"Yes, Ma?"

"Come and get the shopping. We need to make more shortbread and a fresh batch of scones."

"Yes, Ma." The young girl appeared from the back and seized the shopping bags before retreating.

"What the devil do you think you're doing?" she demanded, her gaze including Suzie. "I've been out for one hour, and you've driven away my customers, broken my plates, and spilled tea and milk on the floor."

"They were trying to intimidate your daughter and demanded food and tea," Suzie said. "I merely stepped in to tell them to stop, and they took exception to my interference."

"That's not true," Ruddy Cheeks protested. "We were gonna pay for our food."

"Lie," Suzie said calmly. "Check with your daughter. She'll corroborate my story. I was reading and didn't notice what was happening. Customers were waiting for tables, but the place emptied while I was immersed in my book. These two gentlemen, and I use the term loosely, watched you leave and tried to take advantage of your absence."

"Georgia, ring the police," the woman called, raising her voice. She turned a fierce glare on the two men. "Harold and Timothy Bracewell, your mother would be ashamed of your behavior. God rest her poor soul. Now leave. The police know where to find you, and I'm pressing charges this time."

Suzie fought the need to grin. Well, she sure told them. Both men muttered curses then slunk from the cafe, slamming the door and kicking the sandwich board promoting the specials.

"Good riddance. I planned to be absent for ten minutes, but the bank was busy. Thank you for stepping in to help. Georgia..." She shook her head. "She needs to assert herself."

"I don't like bullies."

"Me neither," the woman said briskly. "Now, can I get you something?"

"No, thanks. I was relaxing after my shopping." And trying to think how to win over a stubborn bear. Or maybe she should kick his butt for thinking the worst of her.

The woman nodded and bustled away, clearing several tables as she went. Suzie returned to her table to drink her last cup of tea. How did one seduce a hard-headed bear determined to place her in the enemy role? She should've been eager to return home and take up her university place. Her shoulders sagged. She'd thought it before, and it was still true—it wouldn't be an adventure without Edwina. They'd been friends forever after meeting at school. She should be angry but couldn't dredge up a scrap of angst because now that she'd met Niall, she understood. Meeting someone with a strong connection didn't happen often.

"Stupid, obstinate bear."

He should hibernate—preferably with her—and get over his dim-witted ways. Suzie didn't know what sort of women he'd been associating with before she came along. Still, they'd either been manipulative or had been the intelligent variety who'd seen this bear's high principles and understood he'd never let a woman into his world.

"What am I going to do?" Suzie muttered.

A yellow teapot landed on her table with a thump, along with a box that—judging by her quick sniff—held baked goodies.

"If the man is worth it, fight for him," the cafe owner said. "If not, do yourself a favor and turn him loose. Life is too short to waste on worthless males."

Suzie grinned at the forthright advice. This was something her father might tell her while her mother worried and stressed. "I'd come to that conclusion myself."

The woman nodded. "Thanks again for aiding Georgia when everyone else left. Typical!"

"You're welcome," Suzie said. "And thanks for the

treats. You didn't need to give me anything."

"I sensed that, which made me decide you deserved a gift." With a brisk nod, the woman marched away.

Suzie smiled after the brusque woman and settled in to drink more tea. By the time she gathered her shopping bags, ready to return to the castle, she was still unsure how to handle Niall. The grumpy bear had gotten to her, and she now understood that beneath his protective shell, this shifter cared deeply for those around him. He had a marshmallow center and was loving and sweet. He was the one she wanted by her side.

At that moment, it felt like an impossible dream. Maybe it was better for her to return home and study her music. At the very least, she'd have firsthand experience of heartbreak, which might help increase her repertoire of songs.

Suzie bid farewell to the cafe owner and her daughter and stepped outside into the late afternoon sun. She wandered along the sidewalk, taking in the other pedestrians and nodding at the various shifters she recognized from the gathering. She decided to do a circuit and window shop when she reached the cobblestone square in the middle of the village. Yeah, she was delaying returning to the castle. She admitted it.

"Hello. Who do we have here?"

For a second, her chest lurched because the man sounded so much like Niall. She swiveled and almost wrenched her ankle on the uneven cobblestones. Niall's brothers. Both wore mischievous expressions that told her they intended to create havoc. How, she wasn't sure, but her gut tightened in alarm.

"What do you want?"

"Our little brother likes you," Colin said, chortling for no reason Suzie could fathom.

She frowned and said nothing.

"You're going to tell us everything you know about Niall and his business," Euan said.

Suzie remained mute while her brain tried to fashion a plan to escape these two idiots. Together, they were stronger than her, but surely they didn't intend to harm her in the middle of a busy square.

"You'll tell us about the security measures at the castle. The men he has hired and his plans for his new honey."

How did they know about Niall's honey? "I can't help you with that. I suggest you approach Niall yourselves."

Euan leaned closer until his breath seared her cheek. Suzie jerked away, trying to avoid the toxic fumes. He reached out a beefy hand and curled it around her biceps, not seeming to care he was hurting her.

"You will tell us, or else," Colin said.

"Or else what?" Perhaps prodding the bear wasn't the best idea, but she didn't intend to help these idiots harm Niall.

Without warning, Colin closed the distance between them and kissed her. She struggled, but his easy strength overpowered her. Two of her packages dropped to the ground. To anyone watching, it'd seem they were a couple, especially when Euan hooted, his cry attracting the attention of bystanders. Suzie gave up fighting, and when Colin relaxed, she kicked him in the shins.

Colin's grip tightened, and he shook her, delight clinging to his features. Bastard. He was a better actor than she'd given him credit for, and she saw several passersby smile, thinking them a romantic couple. *Ugh!* Let him try to kiss her again with that slobbering mouth.

"What do you want from me?" she snarled.

"Just proving a point," Euan said. "So, what's inside these packages?"

"They're presents for my family," Suzie said.

"No honey samples. Pity. We could've done with those."

Suzie froze, her gaze narrowing. "This is about your brother?"

"Runt owes us," Euan said, punctuating this with a growl.

"He owes you nothing."

"He's a Sinclair, but he won't share his riches with us—his kin," Euan said.

"It's his duty," Colin agreed.

Suzie stared at Euan, lost for words. He... They... No wonder Niall preferred to strike out independently rather than stick with his family. They wanted to use his hard work and seize the rewards. No worse, they expected Niall to hand over his earnings without protest merely because he had the misfortune of being born into their family.

"Niall has worked hard to get where he is now," Suzie said, but she could tell these two morons would never see that. They could only see the money at the rainbow's end—Niall's wealth.

"Kiss her again, Colin. Show her who's boss," Euan said without warning.

Colin didn't hesitate. He crushed her to his chest, and despite her physical and verbal protests, he subjected her to another of his slobbery kisses.

"Good job," Euan said when Colin released her.

Suzie glared at them both, then realized Euan wasn't looking at them. He was staring over her shoulder with an expression of utter satisfaction.

13

APOLOGIES

NIALL GAPED AT HIS brothers and Suzie. Colin was kissing her.

His mate.

"Mine. Mine. Mine!" his bear chanted, and the possessive words held a distinct growl.

Suzie was their mate, so why would she kiss Colin with such enthusiasm, their bodies plastered together, chest to chest?

Niall took half a step, his gaze on the couple. He'd come to find Suzie and apologize because he'd been wrong. Unfortunately, his past had intruded, shoving him to the wrong conclusion. Angus had set him straight and told him Suzie had been genuinely upset.

Suzie hadn't met anyone other than to say a casual hello and hadn't made phone calls. Angus had conducted a secondary investigation for him. Suzie was precisely who she professed to be—a shifter from Middlemarch in New Zealand.

Yeah. He owed Suzie a heartfelt apology. But he hadn't expected to witness her kissing his brother. Devastation filled him. Betrayal. Yes, he'd treated her harshly. However, he hadn't anticipated her to run into his brother's arms.

He heard a feminine screech and turned to witness Suzie slapping Colin. Colin bellowed, and fear slithered through Niall, especially when Euan cackled like a hyena. Colin drew back his fist, and Niall started running. He wouldn't make it in time. He knew it, but that didn't stop him from trying.

Niall focused on Suzie. She stilled, sensing the danger. He was too far away to help. Colin wouldn't kill her, but he could injure her.

Suzie murmured something too low for Niall to hear. *Don't taunt him. Colin has no sense of humor. Not a scrap.* Not unless he's carrying out the prank.

Colin released a furious roar and loosed his punch. Suzie dropped, shifting her weight and rocking Colin off balance. His punch skimmed the outside of her arm, and seconds later, Colin fell on his arse.

Euan roared with laughter. Colin cursed up a storm. Niall finally reached the group as Suzie bobbed to her full height and kicked Colin in the ribs. She hadn't noticed him yet, and he wondered what reception he'd receive.

"Never grab me like that again. I feel sorry for the women in your life because you kiss like a wet fish."

"Bitch."

Niall made a choking sound but held his laugh at bay.

He did not need to rile Colin any further. Euan didn't seem to have a problem, probably because he was the oldest brother, and Colin always followed his lead. With a wary gaze on his brothers, he turned his attention to his mate.

His bear hummed a joyful sound, and Niall found his lips curving into a smile as he watched her. He was in awe of her bravery and her cool head.

Suzie picked up her shopping bags and muttered under her breath. He must've made a sound because her head jerked up. "Why are you here?"

Niall went with the truth. "I came to apologize and beg your forgiveness. I want you to come home with me."

"Why the change of heart?"

"I realized I was acting like a fool and jumping to unfair conclusions. You have spent every moment with me."

Suzie's brows rose. "Apart from my walk, where I came across two idiots."

One of his brothers growled, and once again, Niall fought a smile.

"If the cap fits," Suzie snapped.

"I let my past govern good sense," Niall said. "I hope you'll forgive me. At least give me another chance to prove myself to you."

"Oh, brother," Euan said. "She has you under her thumb."

"Your opinion doesn't matter," Niall said. "I'm not the same cub you tormented all those years ago."

Suzie didn't reply. She picked up every bag and turned toward the castle, her strides brisk. Niall fell into step while monitoring his brothers. He didn't stop his watchful manner until he and Suzie were halfway back to the castle.

"Are you speaking to me?"

"I haven't had the best day," Suzie said. "And I'm rather tired of bossy men placing me in the little lady category."

"I haven't done that."

Suzie stopped walking to glare at him. "No, your behavior was worse. You treated me as an equal and accused me of betrayal. You didn't even give me a chance to defend myself."

A flash of shame struck, and Niall hung his head because that was precisely what had happened. He raised his gaze to meet her beautiful green one. "I'm sorry, Suzie. That's exactly what I did. I'll try harder in the future to hold back my temper."

"And you will stop letting your childhood color your reactions. You're an adult. Successful. Smart. Sexy," she added after a pause.

Niall knew then that she'd forgiven him—at least a little. "I am sorry. My brothers..." He hesitated, wondering how much he should tell her.

Everything, his bear chided, and Niall's shoulders slumped momentarily. "Now is not the place, but I'll tell you more about my brothers soon."

"They want your money."

"Of course they do. They never could walk past a bet. They've probably borrowed money from the wrong person and neglected to repay their loans."

Suzie frowned, then surveyed their surroundings. They'd left the main square and taken the road toward the castle. She cast a glance behind them before looking at him.

136

Suzie leaned close enough for him to catch a trace of citrus from her hair.

"Your brothers mentioned your honey. Would they have organized the attempt to acquire your newest product?"

"Euan and Colin are smart. Crafty. They might've made an educated guess since it's not a secret I'm a honey producer. I didn't pick up their scents at my research building. Did you sense anything?"

Suzie's brow puckered. "The intruders had human scents. Nothing distinctive that I recall, although I'd recognize them if I encountered them again."

"Same," Niall said. "Normally, these occurrences wouldn't bother me, but if I add everything together plus the upcoming release date of my product, I'm inclined to increase my security and keep an even closer eye on my brothers."

"I don't blame you. What will you do?"

"The investigator hasn't come back to me yet. If I understood where they fit in this mess, it'd help me decide what to do next."

Suzie's expression softened, and the tightness in Niall's chest reduced.

"I feel as if my world has tipped upside down. Before, everything was easier. Now..." He shrugged, not wanting to seem mushy. But hell. Since Suzie walked into his life, he couldn't think clearly. He snorted inwardly. He wanted to blame his confusion and unease on Suzie when it wasn't her fault. She'd had her life mapped out and wanted different things from him. But it was hard to fight fate.

He didn't even know if he wished to return to his

pre-Suzie life. That had been a lonely existence where he'd had mainly acquaintances rather than friends. He'd immersed himself in work, and since he loved every moment of the challenge, nothing else had mattered. Yes, he'd dated women, but most of those relationships had been disasters. He'd thought he would remain alone—his destiny.

Until Suzie.

"Why are you frowning so hard?"

Niall took his time answering, checking their surroundings as they left the outskirts of the village. "If you had your life planned and no interest in a mate, why did you come to the gathering?"

"I never said I didn't want a mate. I objected to my parents and grandparents dictating my life, thinking they knew better. As for the gathering—I'm sure I've mentioned Saber and London asked Edwina and me to attend. Six of us came from Middlemarch, and they approached us all. Our attendance was voluntary. No one forced us to do anything. All Saber wanted was for shifters to participate with open minds. They didn't put pressure on us and didn't mind if we returned home without a mate. Saber and London thought the experience would benefit us and other younger Middlemarch residents. Some shifters in attendance look desperate because their families have such high expectations."

"Good to know," Niall said.

They walked for a few minutes in companionable silence.

"I gave the go-ahead to put the honey into production

today, but I haven't told anyone this product is special. It's labeled honey and nothing more at this stage. The plain label and reasonable price point should help the honey sell itself. Once people taste it, I'm hoping word of mouth will do the rest."

Niall was pleased to see that Suzie scanned their surroundings before she replied. "You don't want to create a splashy launch and extoll your honey's benefits from the start?"

"All the catchy names and fancy labels won't do a thing if my product sucks."

Suzie laughed, and Niall's steps faltered at the bright, bubbly sound. This woman. She was the whole package. He recalled their night together and fervently wished he hadn't destroyed their fledgling relationship with his bullheadedness.

Suzie... She'd made him feel, made him think, and yeah, she'd made him laugh. For once, he wasn't allowing business to consume him. He wanted her to stay of her own volition. He desired Suzie for himself. Hell, he needed her.

It was time to apologize again.

"Suzie, I'm sorry for jumping to conclusions and forcing you from my home. I wasn't thinking clearly. Our night together put me off balance, and I behaved badly before my brain engaged."

She shot him a look filled with annoyance. "You would've let me go home to New Zealand and done nothing to stop me."

Niall winced because he understood her irritation, and

she had a point. "Suzie, males can be dense sometimes, and I'm worse than most. I'm so sorry." He caught the flicker of doubt in her. She also possessed a core of stubbornness but concealed it beneath her smiling visage. "I know I don't deserve a second chance, but please forgive me."

"Why did you walk and not drive?" she asked suddenly, ignoring his apology.

He'd have to try harder. "I wanted to follow your trail, so walking was easier."

She nodded. "Your brothers are troublemakers. I doubt they're finished with their mischief."

"I'm positive they haven't," Niall said, recalling Colin kissing her. He could smell his brother on her, and that irritated him. "I'll contact the private investigator as soon as we get back. Hopefully, he'll have found something useful because I don't trust their sudden arrival in Scotland."

Suzie handed off her parcels at the castle to a young man who assisted Angus. "Could you leave them in my room for me, please?" She gave him her room number, and Niall went cold.

"I thought you'd move back in with me," he said, watching her carefully.

"I think it's best if I have my own space. Besides, I want to catch up with Liam and Scott. I haven't seen them today."

"Oh." He'd damaged their fledgling relationship with his distrust.

Suzie halted him when he would've turned away. "We're still new to each other, and I don't want to make a hasty decision I'll regret."

Niall felt his mouth drop open and hurriedly corrected his expression. He pressed his lips together and waited. This was his fault. If he didn't stop letting himself get dragged back to that tiny quivering cub covered with bruises and scared of his shadow, he'd never win a beauty like Suzie. She was fierce and independent. Sure of herself and her future, and she didn't deserve to land in the middle of whatever mess his brothers were orchestrating.

"Would you have dinner with me?" When it looked as if she might reject his offer, he said, "Bring your Middlemarch friends with you. I'd enjoy meeting them."

She hesitated before smiling, and the tension inside Niall relaxed. "I'll ask them. Liam has enjoyed checking out the old weapons on display. You have a few in your private apartments that I'm sure he'll get excited about viewing."

"Shall we say seven for dinner?"

"Thank you."

Niall's phone buzzed. "Sorry."

"Answer it. I'll see you later."

Niall picked up the call but watched Suzie until she vanished.

"Sinclair? You there?"

"I'm here," Niall said, recognizing the private investigator. From his terse tone, he had information. "What have you got for me?"

14

TEAM NIALL

"D INNER? WITH THE GUY that owns this place?" Scott asked.

"Yes," Suzie said, unable to hold back her blush. "He...I..." She trailed off, unsure of how to explain their relationship.

Liam sidled closer and sniffed her. He grinned and winked at Scott. "I think they've cuddled because she smells of bear."

The heat intensified in Suzie's cheeks.

"Suzie, do you have something to tell us?" Scott asked, his green eyes twinkling with mischief.

"No," she blurted. Too quickly because the men's grins widened. "All right," she snapped. "He's my mate. At least I'm fairly sure we're mates. It's so confusing. He's confusing."

Liam lost his teasing grin. "From what I've heard, it's

different for every couple. For some, the knowledge is intuitive, while for others, one party experiences the pull stronger than the other. There is no rhyme or reason behind nature."

"That's baffling," Suzie said, sighing loudly. If Edwina were here, she'd discuss this with her, but Liam and Scott were the last ones standing. "I like Niall, not because he's wealthy and a successful businessman. I can talk with him about dozens of topics and not get bored."

"What about the sex?" Scott asked.

"I'm not talking about that with—okay. Fine. The sex was fantastic, but the next day, he accused me of working with his brothers and giving away sensitive business information. And before you ask, I didn't do that. His product is amazing, and I'd never sneak info to his competitors. *Never.* Niall has worked hard to gain his success." Aware she was prattling, she stopped to glower at her grinning male friends. "Laugh it up, boys. Do you want to come to dinner or not?"

"Yes," Scott said.

"Wouldn't miss it," Liam agreed.

"We wouldn't ignore a dinner summons," Scott said, and her eyes narrowed when his lips quivered.

"We want to check out this mate of yours," Liam said. "And report back to Saber and London."

Her squinty-eyed glare did little to curb Liam's humor at her expense. "Please don't humiliate me," she said.

"We won't," Scott said earnestly, but she didn't believe him. If she stood in his shoes, she'd be teasing him or Liam full-out.

She harrumphed, but they were making a point of not returning her gaze. "If either of you embarrass me, remember payback is a bitch. I'll meet you at the entrance."

"The lobby with the cool swords and shields on the walls?" Liam asked.

Suzie nodded. "Yes. Ten to seven, okay? I'm going to have a drink and see what's happening in the great hall. Coming?"

Scott shuddered. "Liam and I are walking to the village for some time out. I've had two propositions today and one marriage proposal."

Suzie blinked and glanced at Liam to see if Scott was dramatizing events.

Liam scowled, his green eyes flashing a hint of anger. "Suzie, he's not kidding. Two male shifters hit on me at breakfast. I had a female lion grab and kiss me while her friends took photographic proof, and two shifters from our corridor broke into our room. I didn't hear them, which was weird, but one climbed into bed with me before I was properly awake. It is a jungle out there. You'll see."

"You're exaggerating," Suzie scoffed, but neither male cracked a grin.

"See you later," Scott said with a wave.

Suzie gazed after the two men and shook her head. "No, it can't be that bad. They're pulling my leg."

Curses!

It was worse, and the way the shifters sniffed at her left her edgy and full of anxiety. And that was in the five minutes she spent in line to grab a cup of tea.

"Back up," she snapped to the couple behind her. They had fair hair and similar features, marking them as siblings. "I'm not interested."

When a wolf shifter prowled along the line, pausing at several women, Suzie decided she didn't want tea that badly. She'd settle for a bottle of water. Suzie stomped past the wolf shifter and ignored his rumbly voice as he tried to flirt with her.

"Come back, baby. I can light your fire," he said.

Gah! No wonder he was single and desperate. If she'd still had Edwina as her wingman, she might've stopped to give him a few pointers. But she wasn't feeling that magnanimous today. She had enough problems of her own.

Suzie grabbed a beverage from the ice bucket on the bar and headed outside to the garden. It wasn't as pretty as the private gardens on Niall's side of the castle, but it was relatively peaceful. The MC had organized a scavenger hunt, and Suzie found a quiet bench, content to listen to the competitors' merriment and frustration.

Her thoughts slipped to Niall, and she wondered if they had a future or if his distrust would drive them apart. He'd already been on edge because of his honey and the break-in at his facility. Suzie understood why he'd jumped to the conclusions he had, but his distrust had hurt. She'd given him her virginity, and she'd thought he'd understood this meant she was all in with him.

She'd never betray him. No, she was Team Niall. At least he'd seen his brother kiss her and witnessed her reaction. His older brothers were creepy.

A rustle in the bushes to her right made her start, and she cursed herself for letting her guard down. Any shifter sneaking up and thinking to score with her could think again. She wasn't interested.

Rustling came from the nearby bushes, and she realized the group had moved to another area of the castle grounds. Gradually, she relaxed because she couldn't scent anything in the wind. The birds had ceased their twittering momentarily, but everything reverted to normal. Reassured, Suzie went back to thinking about Niall.

The sun was warm on her skin, and she closed her eyes. *Not safe!* She jerked upright and forced herself to full wakefulness a second before someone seized her shoulders. They pressed a smelly cloth to her nose.

Panicked, Suzie struggled, but they were too strong. She sucked in a huge breath and wished she hadn't because someone had soaked the cloth with a drug of some type. She thrashed, jerking her arms and legs and trying to get leverage to spring to her feet while holding her breath.

The person—or was it two people—held her easily.

"Stop fighting," a gruff voice demanded.

Suzie didn't waste her breath on a reply, more concerned with ripping the cloth off her nose. Her lungs ached, crying for oxygen. Her vision went dark around the edges, and she broke, gasping and desperate for a proper lungful of air. The sickly, sweet scent filled her senses, and instead of helping, it made Suzie slip toward an inky blackness.

"That's my girl," a masculine voice crooned. "Suck it in. No one will hurt you. We need your help."

What help? Suzie's limbs became heavy, and she slumped forward. Firm hands halted her from face-planting on the gravel.

"Don't feel well." The words emerged as garbled nonsense. Suzie fell deeper into the darkness until nothing else existed.

15

MISSING

NIALL DIDN'T START WORRYING until it was a quarter past the hour. He searched for Angus and discovered him with two young men at the public entrance to the castle.

He glanced around expectantly and frowned. "Where's Suzie?"

The young men turned to him, seemingly surprised.

"We thought she must be with you," one said, his green eyes narrowed in his tanned face.

The other said, "Suzie is never late. She told us she'd meet us here." He was taller, and a nasty scar disfigured his face. Despite this, his gaze, more blue than green, was steady.

"When did you see her last?" Niall asked.

"When she invited us to dinner. She found us at the bar, then left for fresh air. She told us she intended to stay close to the castle," Liam said, his frown lopsided because of his scar.

"Did she tell you why?" Niall demanded.

"No." Scott's dark brows drew together. "Is Suzie in danger?"

Niall didn't answer but turned to Angus. "Have you sent someone to check her room?"

"She's not there. Scott and I stopped by her room since we're on the same floor. I'm Liam. This is Scott."

"Niall," Niall said, worry threading through him as he called the private investigator. "Have you got eyes on my brothers?" He didn't wait for the man to speak. "My girlfriend is missing."

"I called my men off after I spoke to you. Do you want me to locate them again?"

"Please. Call if you find them." Niall hung up. "Which part of the garden did she go to?

"She likes roses," Scott said.

Liam nodded in agreement. "It might be possible to track her, but they had a scavenger hunt during the afternoon. The other shifters' scents might muddy the trail."

"Let's go," Niall said.

"I'll organize a search of the castle," Angus called after him.

"Thank you." Niall hastened outside with Scott and Liam a few steps behind. Concern and suspicion stabbed him as he strode past the castle chapel, the gravel crunching beneath his shoes. He tried hard to push his apprehension away but didn't succeed. Her friends were worried about her, and this made his gut churn harder.

The garden was empty in the evening as most gathering shifters readied for dinner and pre-dinner drinks.

"Let's split up," Scott suggested. "We can cover more ground that way."

The three men searched in different directions. Niall's heart jumped when he stumbled across her scent. *His mate.*

Somehow, he had to force his brothers to return home. Everything had been fine until their arrival. The thought tickled his brain as he carefully followed the scent trail.

He halted abruptly when the thought solidified. His issues with his honey had begun when his brothers arrived. The investigator's report hadn't turned up any links, but the facts fit the scenario. Someone had contacted his family and learned about their estrangement, or his brothers had encountered them here in Scotland. Perhaps in a pub, when liquid courage had fueled their tongues. He could picture the scene. Euan and Colin acting indignant about their ungrateful younger brother who refused to acknowledge them or offer them shelter in his castle.

The scent trail ended at a bench overlooking one of the more extensive rose gardens. Niall walked in a wide circle around the bench, his nose quivering. *Ammonia. Bleach.* He backed up, his bear forcing him to sneeze. His eyes streamed, and his suspicions rose. Someone had purposely sprayed the ground, knowing he'd investigate.

Niall wiped his eyes and surveyed the area. Now that he'd smelled the bleach, he could discern nothing else. The disgusting scent dominated everything. Niall held his sleeve to his nose while he searched for clues.

Scott and Liam arrived together.

"Find anything?" Liam called.

"Suzie sat on this bench. I can't find a trail because someone sprayed the ground with bleach and ammonia."

"Where?" Liam asked. "I can't smell it from here."

"That side." Niall gestured right.

The two men headed in that direction, their gazes intent while Niall searched around the bench. Something glinted in the grass. Niall plucked it off the ground. It was Suzie's watch.

"She was here," Niall called. "I've found her watch."

"We've got her phone," Liam said.

Niall trotted over, holding his breath when he neared the sprayed region. The area was more extensive than he'd assumed, and his eyes were watering badly when he reached the men.

Scott grasped Niall's arm. "This way."

Niall followed mindlessly, allowing Scott to guide him.

"I think we're clear," Scott said finally. "The smell doesn't bother us as much."

"I've found signs of a group walking this way," Liam said. "It might be someone from the gathering. It's hard to tell."

Niall wiped his eyes. "Let's follow the trail, anyway. It's the only clue we have."

The scent led to the estate wall. A dirt road lay on the other side, and they concluded someone had whisked Suzie away in a vehicle. Dispirited, Niall led the way back to the castle.

"Did you find Miss Suzie?" Angus asked.

"Someone has taken her," Niall said.

"Why?" Angus asked.

"It's something to do with my new honey," Niall replied. "It's the only thing that makes sense."

Liam frowned. "Why is Suzie's disappearance related to your honey?"

"Yeah," Scott said.

Niall hesitated because he seldom shared information. He learned the hard way when an ex-employee stole a formula for a competitor. Niall hadn't seen the man since, but he'd heard he was still working for the opposition. "I'll have to get you to sign a non-disclosure agreement," he said finally.

Liam snorted.

"Really?" Scott said, scowling.

"A non-disclosure means nothing," Liam snapped. "If Suzie is in danger, we need to move fast. Now."

Niall straightened, irritated at how they'd brushed off his demands. He ground his teeth together to halt the quick words he wanted to spew and forced himself to pause.

Liam and Scott stared at him, their expressions set.

It was a standoff.

Finally, Liam said, "You don't know us, but you know Suzie. She is honest and loyal and would never sell out a friend. It's easy to see you're more than friends. Suzie is an excellent judge of character, and she doesn't take crap from anyone. For her to spend time with you, you must be decent. We're loyal to Suzie because we know and trust her. We're not sure about you, but because of Suzie, we're willing to give you the benefit of the doubt. I'm sure you're worried about her, and that's why you're acting like a moron. Scott and I are farmers. We have ties to New Zealand and want to return home. Besides having it on our morning toast, we're not interested in your honey. Let us help you find Suzie."

Niall studied the man with his scarred face. His blue-green eyes blazed with sincerity, and when Niall turned to Scott, he wore a similar expression. He trusted Suzie. At least, he did now. After a lengthy and fraught pause, he dipped his head.

"All right. This is what I know." He explained about his brothers, how they'd turned up, and his relationship with them. He described his business and his recent problems.

When he finished, Scott said, "Your honey sounds amazing. I hope we can sample it before we return home."

"Do you think they'll hurt Suzie?" Liam asked.

Niall frowned. "If my brothers have her—I don't think they'd hurt a woman, but I haven't seen them since I was fourteen and left home. They're motivated by greed and money."

"You said the private investigator has been checking into them. Do they have gambling debts at home or something like that?" Scott asked.

"That might change the situation if they were desperate to repay debts," Liam said.

"That's what worries me," Niall said. "Especially since they've been known to gamble."

Angus tapped on the door and entered. "A young boy

gave the housekeeper this note when he and his boss delivered a load of meat to the kitchen. He told me a man had paid him ten pounds to deliver it."

Niall's breath seized before he opened the envelope with trembling fingers. Part of the note comprised letters cut from a newspaper. They formed two sentences: Give *me a jar of your honey for the girl. Midnight tonight at the far end of the lake.* Someone else had added in handwriting below this, *plus two hundred thousand pounds in cash.*

16

YOU'RE CRIMINALS

SUZIE JOLTED AWAKE, HER mouth so dry she had to swallow four times before anything happened. Thirst was a nagging craving, and it affected her thought processes. Where was she?

Memories came crashing down on her without warning. She tried to sit up and flapped about like an ungainly fish because someone had bound her feet and her hands behind her back. Suzie ceased wriggling and took a deep breath to counteract the panic gathering in her.

Someone had drugged her.

Euan and Colin. She'd thought she'd caught a whiff of their scents before someone had clapped that stinky cloth over her nose.

In the dark room, Suzie couldn't make out much. She got the impression of furniture, dust, and decay. A deserted building, perhaps?

Footsteps sounded outside the room. Suzie tensed. Dithered. Should she pretend to be asleep, or should she hurl insults at her captors and scream for help? At the last second, she feigned unconsciousness. She could always magically awaken if she judged that wiser.

Suzie closed her eyes not a second too soon. The door flew open. Her heart leaped, adrenaline surging through her. She fought the urge to give her visitor a tongue-lashing.

Their scent gave them away. Colin and Euan. Niall's brothers were causing trouble again, and it was no wonder a younger Niall had given up on his family and left home. It must've been difficult for him at the start, and she respected him for the success he'd made of his life. It made her even more determined to help him get his honey to market.

Footsteps came closer, and a lamp switched on. Suzie found it difficult not to lash out with a pithy diatribe about why Colin and Euan were useless individuals.

"She should be awake by now," Euan murmured, his voice sounding close. *Too close.* "I thought the boss said it was a weak dose and wouldn't hurt her."

Suzie stopped herself from giving an indignant sniff. He sounded as if he cared.

"Doesn't matter," Colin said. "She's breathing, right? As long as she's alive, we have a bargaining chip. We can't fail."

Euan sighed. "Yeah, you're right. We have half our payment. Ma should've paid off our debt by now."

"We should've kept some back and booked a room in a

decent hotel."

Whiny brat. Distaste flowed through Suzie, but she remained still. Niall was worth ten of his siblings. He never acted as if the world owed him. He'd worked hard and forged his path. Suzie hesitated, wondering if she should pretend unconsciousness for longer or magically awaken. No, she'd try to learn more first. Like, who was this mysterious boss who'd issued orders?

"What are we gonna do? We need information, or we won't receive the rest of our money," Colin said.

Huh! You and me both, buddy. Suzie relaxed and settled in to wait for them to discuss their situation. She hoped her bladder got with the program and didn't force her to beg for a restroom.

Much to her disappointment, Euan and Colin fell silent, although Colin, judging by the waft of scent, was driving her up the wall with his incessant pacing. Time passed so slowly she wanted to scream, and finally, she'd had enough. Her eyes flew open, taking precious seconds to adjust.

"I knew it," Colin cried. "You were pretending."

"Arsehole," Suzie spat, not bothering to deny his accusation. He hadn't known at all, otherwise, he wouldn't have paced like a caged animal.

When the two bear shifters stared at her, she growled, the catlike sound making them both flinch.

"Are you intending to explain your actions?" she asked, not holding back on the snark. While she waited for a reply, she scanned the room. The furniture was unloved, with broken legs and frayed upholstery. A thick layer of dust covered every surface, and Colin's footprints were easily discernible. A ratty, sheer curtain covered the sole window. It was high up and not an easy method of escape. The door, then.

The brothers exchanged a glance. Neither spoke.

"I'll begin," Suzie said. "Why have you kidnapped me? And why am I trussed like a Christmas turkey?" The rope binding her feet had loosened slightly with her wriggling. She'd keep them talking while subtly trying to free herself.

"You smell like my brother," Euan said.

Suzie's heart skipped a beat, but she controlled her expression. *Because they were mates.* Yeah, she'd fought this, but her inner soul understood the truth. Niall was her mate, which meant—if she survived the experience with these two dunderheads—she'd stay in Scotland and wouldn't get to take up the scholarship she'd worked so hard to win. She hesitated, instinct telling her to lie.

"Because we decided to have fun together and share a bed until I fly home next week." Good grief. So much had happened to her and her friends during the gathering. They'd need to organize a reunion to catch up. That thought brought a frown because she still hadn't spoken to Edwina. She hoped her friend was safe and she'd truly found a mate.

"You're sleeping with him?" Disbelief sounded in Colin.

"Why not? We're single without ties. He's rich and attractive. A fantastic lover." She met Colin's gaze and then Euan's. Although every word was accurate, what she liked most about Niall was the true heart he hid beneath his grumpy exterior. Despite the knocks he'd received as a youngster, he'd come out the other side. Niall was all that was decent. She paused. And he was a considerate and fantastic lover.

"You're with him for the money," Colin said.

Let them think that. She didn't care because it wasn't the truth. One didn't need money to be happy. Happiness came from small things. Friendship. Love. A touch of hands. Togetherness.

"Why am I here?" Suzie ground out, impatient with the two gawking idiots.

The brothers exchanged a glance before turning back to her.

"You're going to write a note to Niall," Euan said.

Suzie held up her bound hands. "How?"

Euan had the audacity to roll his eyes. "We'll untie your hands."

"Excellent," Suzie muttered. The rope binding her feet was almost loose enough for her to slip one foot free.

"Don't you be getting no ideas of escape," Colin warned. "It's two of us against you." He sniffed. "You're a kitty cat. Bet you transform to something small and scrawny. A lap pet."

Suzie bared her teeth, but that was her only reaction.

"Get the paper and pen," Euan ordered.

Colin stalked over to the other side of the room and fumbled with a brown paper bag. He returned, carrying two pens and a lined pad.

"Why should I write a note to Niall?"

Euan's eyes flared amber before settling back into plain

brown. "Because if you don't, you're not leaving this room alive."

Suzie made a scoffing sound that echoed in the locked room. "You won't hurt me. If anything happens to me, Niall will go to the authorities."

"I thought you said you and Niall are casual lovers," Colin said. "Why would he care if anything happened to you?"

"Because he doesn't claw over others to get ahead." A subtle dig. Too subtle since neither of the bears even blinked.

Interesting. They didn't consider their actions immoral or outside of the law. As far as they were concerned, every penny Niall earned belonged to them. Anger flooded Suzie. Sorrow, too, for the small bear who couldn't fight back, so he'd left and found another family in a lonely old Highlander.

But Niall wasn't content to kick back and spend his inherited money. He continued to work. Although he hadn't told her, it was clear Niall donated some of his spoils and allowed the shifters to use the castle for the gathering.

"You disgust me," Suzie snapped, not holding back her ire. The rope around her wrists snapped.

"Crap," Colin said, freezing, his eyes wide when she kicked one foot free.

"Grab her," Euan ordered.

Colin snapped out of his shock and pounced. He grasped her, and she lashed out with her fingernails, gouging lines on his meaty forearm. He cursed up a storm. Suzie instinctively elbowed him in the guts and stomped on his foot. While he swore and hopped ungainly, she kneed him in the balls and silently thanked Isabella and her take-no-prisoners training. Anger flooded her, counteracting her previous distress.

Euan's brows rose as he observed his younger brother writhing on the floor. "You can't get past me to escape, and I'm not leaving this room until I have your letter."

Suzie thought quickly. They weren't telling her why they wanted this letter. Maybe she'd cooperate and lull them into a false sense of security. Even if they left her alone, locked in this room, she thought she could pick the lock or use her strength to break down the door.

"What will happen after I write the letter?" she asked.

"We'll keep you locked in here while we deliver it to Niall. We'll release you once he follows our instructions."

"What's stopping me from going to the cops?"

An expression of shock slid across Euan. "You'd turn us into the human cops?"

"In a heartbeat. You're criminals, and I bet you entered the country illegally."

He didn't react much, but she caught the twitch of his eye and knew she was right. He wanted nothing to do with the law.

"How did you get into the UK?" she prodded.

"Friends with a boat," he said.

"Ah. So once Niall does whatever you want, you'll disappear until you need more money. Then you'll find another way to extort his wealth."

Euan ignored that dig, too, but Suzie sensed the truth of

her words. To them, Niall would always be the runt and someone for them to bully. They held no respect for his accomplishments. For him.

"Enough," Colin snarled.

Euan prodded the paper and pen toward her. "Write."

Suzie gave a long-suffering sigh. "Very well. What do you want me to write in this oh-so-important letter?"

"Write this: They want to exchange me for your honey and reschedule your product release date until next year. Bring the honey to the end of the lake at ten tonight. If you fail to comply or contact the authorities, you'll not see me again."

Suzie lifted her head to frown at Euan. "I told you I'm flying home next week. If you check with the airline, you'll find I'm booked on the Air New Zealand flight from Heathrow. Niall doesn't have feelings for me. We're friends, that's all."

"I don't believe you," Euan said. "Finish the letter."

Suzie shrugged. "Don't say I didn't tell you."

She continued to write, not using Euan's precise wording, but it was close enough and meant the same thing. Now that she knew her kidnapper's identity, she wasn't as frightened. No, they'd irked her fiercely, and she longed to knock their heads together. She handed over the note and watched Euan read it. Satisfaction slid over his smarmy face, and she trembled with the urge to strike out physically.

Suzie batted down her fury, and once she'd forced her muscles to relax during a casual stretch, she focused on information gathering. "I've told you Niall and I are nothing more than friends. We've enjoyed ourselves with a vacation fling, and that's all we'll ever have."

She silently apologized to Niall because their night together had been everything. She missed him like crazy.

"If you want to believe otherwise, this cluster is on you. Now go away. I'm tired, and I want to sleep." She stood and went to the room's largest, most comfortable-looking chair. A spring jabbed her in the back when she plonked onto the dusty cushion. It was difficult to hide her grimace.

"You're a cool one," Colin said. "I thought you might cry the entire time. Blubber like a baby." He shot a glance at his brother, and Suzie didn't have to be a mind reader to interpret his thoughts.

Colin was speculating if they'd made a colossal mistake. He was wondering if they had the wrong lever to make their little brother follow their orders. And most of all, he was questioning whether she was telling the truth.

17

SEARCH FOR SUZIE

"NIALL, A BOY DELIVERED this note for you," Angus said, bursting into his study with barely a pause to knock. Most unAnguslike.

"Thanks, Angus," Niall said.

Liam and Scott sat across his desk, their expressions holding tension.

Niall ripped open the envelope and read the message before handing it over to the shifters. "Is that Suzie's handwriting?"

"Yes," Scott said.

"Will they hurt her?" Liam demanded. "I take it they want your miracle honey."

"That's my assumption, but I could give them any old honey and label it with my new packaging. As to hurting her—I don't know."

"Will you bring in the cops?" Liam asked. "That's what

we'd do at home, but they're part of the shifter circle even though our cops are human."

Niall considered this and nodded. "I think I should contact them and make this official."

Scott and Liam radiated approval, and Niall appreciated their support.

"We'll keep searching while you deal with the cops," Liam said. "They must have Suzie somewhere local. That's what I'd do."

"Yeah," Scott said. "It would make sense that they'd want to monitor you and control the situation."

Glad to have these two men to run ideas, Niall reached for the phone. Their presence helped to keep the edge off his panic. He didn't care about his honey—not when Suzie was in danger. He could develop a new product, and that told him everything. Suzie was the critical part of this equation. Her safety.

"Do you have any idea who would snatch her?" Scott asked.

"Yeah, normally people kidnap to obtain money. Honey seems a strange substitute," Liam said.

"Not if you knew how much money went into research and development. The health benefits surpass anything I've witnessed, and no additives is the most astonishing aspect."

"Your first suspects are your brothers, right?" Liam asked.

Niall inclined his head.

"Would they want your honey?" Liam asked. "You had a private investigator on them. What made you do that?"

Liam was right. "My brothers wouldn't understand how valuable my honey was unless someone told them. I haven't seen my family since leaving Canada. I made no secret of my whereabouts, so locating me wouldn't have been difficult."

Scott leaned forward, his gaze intent. "Did you ask them why they came? Why they sought you out?"

"They wanted money."

"Did they say why?" Liam asked.

"No, but the private investigator uncovered gambling debts. My brothers are enthusiastic but unsuccessful gamblers. They borrowed from a loan shark, and their loan is overdue. I assume they thought I'd give them money because they're family."

"Right, that makes more sense than the honey. Who else would want your honey? Have you had any other security problems?" Scott asked.

"Yes," Niall said, thinking they were right. The honey part didn't fit neatly. "A break-in occurred at our development premises where we mix and blend different honey. Only my foreman and I work here. Few people are aware of the location. It isn't even on the map."

"Security cameras?" Liam asked.

"Someone disabled them. We caught flashes of masked men before they sprayed the cameras with black paint. Nothing else."

"What did they take?" Liam asked.

"Some honey, but they didn't get the right one because I always mislabel it and pack it away with pots of common clover or heather honey. We place a special code on the

166

label that no one else would notice during a quick search."

"What about your notes and things like that?" Scott asked.

"We assume they copied the production notes but nothing else to help them. I lock my private notes away or hide them. Sometimes, I'll take them home to work in my office there."

"Who would benefit from stealing your formula or stopping you from selling your honey?" Liam asked. "That is where we should look."

"I can compile a list of competitors," Niall said.

"You should do that," Scott said. "Give it to the cops but mention your brothers and their debts. If the cops can catch your brothers, they might deport them."

Niall grinned, and it wasn't a nice, friendly one. He liked the idea of getting his brothers tossed from his adopted country perhaps a little too much. His bear chuffed in agreement.

"There is another possibility," Scott said, his forehead scrunched in concentration. "What if your brothers were working for one of your competitors? You refused to hand over money, and this might be retaliation. They get their money, plus they get the satisfaction of taking your woman."

The phone rang.

"Yes," Niall spoke tersely.

"We've located your brothers again," the private investigator said. "They haven't moved locations."

"Thank you," Niall said. "Can you hold for a couple of secs?" He glanced at Liam and Scott. "Want to join me in searching for Suzie?"

"Hell, yeah," Scott said.

Niall nodded and returned to his call. "Where are they? I'll be there in around ten to fifteen minutes."

The investigator gave Niall directions.

"Right," Niall said. "Let's see if Suzie is with them. If she isn't, I'll contact the cops."

Scott checked his watch. "If it isn't your brothers, we'll still have time to meet with the kidnappers."

The two men hopped into a vehicle with Niall and set off to meet the investigator. Judging by the PI's directions, his brothers were staying on the village outskirts, but he didn't recognize the street.

He pulled up behind a black SUV and cut the engine. "The investigator suggested we meet here and go on foot," Niall said.

"Does he know we're shifters?" Scott asked.

"No."

"How about you keep him distracted?" Liam asked. "We'll approach in feline form because we know Suzie's scent."

"My brothers will smell you coming," Niall warned.

"They haven't noticed the humans keeping watch on them," Scott pointed out.

Niall brightened because this was true. "They're probably arrogant enough to think no one can touch them."

"The shifter scents might be a disadvantage, so we should take care," Liam said. "Let's locate Suzie first, then strategize her retrieval."

Scott flashed a smile. "That makes Suzie sound like a parcel. She won't like that."

Niall imagined his Suzie and grinned, his heart lightening at the thought. Scott was right. She would draw herself up and become indignant and stroppy. Her sexy green eyes would flash salvos of wrath. A chuckle emerged.

Scott slapped him over the back. "Braver man than me."

"We'd better go," Liam said.

"I'll distract the investigator." Niall climbed out of his vehicle and jogged to the driver's side of the SUV. Suzie had to be all right. If his brothers had hurt her...

The investigator wound down his window, his white cotton shirt crisp despite the heat and his brown eyes bright with intelligence. "It's the old white bungalow on the left—almost falling down."

"Thanks," Niall said.

"What do you intend to do?" the investigator asked. His shrewd brown eyes were the only exceptional thing about him, the rest of him ordinary and unassuming, which made him an excellent detective. He was a man who never panicked.

"I'll check to see if they have my girlfriend, and if they do, they'll regret it." Niall might've been the runt during his early life, but the old man who'd taken him in had helped to build his confidence. He'd honed his strength and trained in different self-defense methods until it became second nature. He didn't fear his brothers. Now, they plain irritated him, and especially their assumption that they still had the upper hand. He'd disabuse them of that soon enough.

"Who are those men with you?" the investigator inquired.

"They're from New Zealand. Suzie's friends," Niall said, amused. Yep, the man missed nothing.

"Do you need help?"

"Thanks, but no. We'll be fine. Also, my brothers need to take care of Suzie. She's no wilting flower."

The older man grinned. "They're the best sort. My missus is the same. When you find one like that, it's best to keep them. I'll put my bill in the mail."

"Thank you," Niall said.

The SUV started, and the investigator pulled away with a wave.

Niall waited until the engine's rumble faded before he strode toward the property. His original plan was to sneak around and peer through windows, but he decided against it. He lengthened his stride and bounded up the three steps leading to the front door. The wood had cracked and—from its looks—warped from water damage. Red paint peeled from the surface, sending a shower of flecks flying when he pounded his fist on the door.

Niall stopped and waited, cocking his head to better listen for sounds within. Nothing. His chest grew tight, and an ache sprang to life in his jaw. Niall forced himself to relax his mouth and take a breath. When he faced his brothers, he required calmness to help Suzie. Yep, time to quash his anger, his frustration. This was not the moment to revert to the bullied young child.

Niall hammered on the door again, and footsteps became audible when he paused. Except they were behind him. He whirled around, his eyes widening. "You!" He took half a step before a blow to the head felled him.

18

DON'T LET HIM DIE

THE KERFUFFLE DRAGGED SUZIE to the keyhole.
Had Niall found her, or was something else
happening? Dang, they'd built these walls thick. Someone
was shouting or cursing. It was difficult to hear the actual
words. Stumped, she returned to the lone seat and sat.
That lasted for three seconds because the restless energy
pulsing through her veins forced her to jump to her feet.
Edgy and conflicted, she paced the room, unable to fashion
an escape plan.

Euan and Colin were immense and robust in their
human forms. While she was fast, she doubted she'd
dart past the two of them and make it outside without
recapture. She knew nothing of the building's layout—a
considerable disadvantage when trying to flee.

Hearing a loud crash, she froze, then stared at the door,
almost as if she could see through it. What was happening

out there?

Suzie searched for a makeshift weapon. She could always hit her captors with one of the many moldy books. She was a decent bowler when they played backyard cricket at home. Suzie gathered and placed the discarded books on a rickety coffee table. And none too soon. The key rattled in the lock, and someone flung the door open. Suzie hurled the first book before she second-guessed herself.

Colin released a grunt. "Stop that."

Suzie tossed the next book and gasped when it struck Niall in the face. A silent, unresponsive Niall. Pages fell from the binding, thumping onto the floor.

Colin bared his teeth as he dropped Niall, stepped back, and slammed the door. Seconds later, the key turned.

Suzie raced to Niall's side. He hadn't moved, hadn't so much as twitched when he struck the floor. She fumbled to check his pulse, her fingers trembling as she placed them on the side of his neck. Relief hit her with a whoosh. He had a heartbeat, and now that her panic had receded, she could see the steady rise of his chest. But the blood. It trickled down his cheek. A book shouldn't have caused that type of damage. With careful fingers, she turned his head. On the right side, blood matted his hair, and she gingerly touched the area. He didn't flinch, but her fingers came away red. Someone else had struck him on the head. His brothers?

Colin was usually talkative, even if it was annoying. He'd seemed angry when he dumped Niall in the room with her. Angry at Niall for coming to get her or for another reason?

The key turned, and the door opened.

It was Colin again. He flung a stack of cloth at her. "Look after him. We don't want him to die."

"Then you shouldn't have hit him," Suzie snapped. "Call a doctor. You shouldn't mess around with head wounds."

"No doctor. Euan and I don't have any shifter contacts. You'll have to do your best."

"Wait. What's going on?" Suzie asked.

"A major clusterfuck," Colin snarled and slammed the door in her face.

"Well, that was helpful." Suzie gathered the fabric strips he'd tossed in her direction. She wondered what had Colin's knickers in a twist. What had gone wrong with their planning? Niall wouldn't give them money because he wasn't a stupid man. He understood they'd keep coming back. They'd gamble away everything they had and keep going if he enabled them. Niall would never get rid of them.

Shouting came from behind the door, followed by a bear-like growl. While there weren't any near neighbors, someone might hear and call the police if they continued with that racket. Suzie stood to retrieve the water bottle she'd discovered in the room. She moistened the cloth and cleaned the cut on Niall's head. From what she'd heard, head wounds bled a lot, but surely the bleeding should've slowed, given Niall's shifter status.

She turned another cloth strip into a pad and pressed it against the wound. That might help to slow or stop the bleeding. He'd created quite a puddle.

The shouts continued, combined with a crash or two.

Loud footsteps came closer, and she tensed as the scrape of a key signaled someone was incoming.

Euan stood in the doorway. From her spot on the floor beside Niall, she observed another man standing in the shadows. He was keeping to the background, but she suspected he might be the one pulling their strings. She scooted a few inches away from Niall, trying to see the stranger's face. He retreated before she got a clear view. The man wasn't overly large, nor was he short. He wore black trousers and a button-down shirt rather than the T-shirts Niall's brothers sported.

Euan shut the door and locked it at a curt order from the man. Frowning, Suzie returned to Niall's side. His breathing was even, and the bleeding seemed to have stopped, but she didn't like the paleness of his face. As a shifter, he should heal rapidly. All she could do was make him comfortable while hoping he'd regain consciousness soon.

Sighing, Suzie curled beside Niall, sharing her body heat with him. She tried to make a plan and discarded every idea that came to her as unworkable. She must've fallen asleep because she jolted awake when a big hand grasped her shoulder.

"Shush, lass. It's me," Niall said. "Are you all right? Did they hurt you?"

"I'm fine." The tension seeped out of Suzie, and she pushed to a sitting position, every muscle protesting. "How is your head?"

"I have a low-grade headache," Niall said.

"What's the time?"

Niall checked his watch. "Almost three. I heard voices outside."

"Your brothers?"

"I don't think so."

"Niall? Suzie?" a familiar masculine voice shouted.

"You can't go in there, sir. Wait outside," another man said, annoyance simmering in his tone.

"That sounds like Scott and Liam." Suzie climbed to her feet and groaned. "Remind me not to sleep on the floor again."

"It's not so bad," Niall said, rising with a grimace. "I woke with you pressed to my side. I can think of worse ways to wake."

"Silver tongue."

"Hello. Is anyone here?" a man called.

"We're here," Niall said in a calm voice. "We're locked in."

"There's no key," came the reply.

"Bastards took it with them," Suzie said. "Just wait until I see your brothers again. I'll knock their heads together."

"We'll have to catch them first," Niall said, "but I'll hold them for you when we do."

Pleasure poured through Suzie, and she fluttered her lashes, knowing he'd see even in the low light. "Thank you. I can't wait."

"Stand back," the man said. "We'll break down the door."

She and Niall retreated. A loud thump came, followed by a swift curse.

"Where is Evans?" the man demanded.

More voices came, then a crash. The wood split and the lock creaked before the door burst open. A large man in a police uniform filled the entrance, and Suzie got a whiff of wolf shifter before he stood back and allowed others to enter.

"Mr. Sinclair and Ms. Paisley?" a plain-clothes policeman asked.

"Yes," Niall said.

"Are you injured?" the wolf shifter asked. He must've smelled the blood.

"They hit Niall over the head," Suzie said. "It's stopped bleeding now, but he should probably get it looked at."

"All right. Evans, you have first-aid training. You look at Mr. Sinclair's head while I interview Ms. Paisley. The other room has better light and chairs."

The policeman asked his questions, and Suzie talked more than usual because she saw Evans speaking to Niall in a low voice. Since he was a shifter, it was best if Niall talked to him.

"Did you recognize anyone?" the policeman asked Suzie.

"Yes," Niall said, limping over to join them. "Two of my brothers—Euan and Colin. There was someone else. The man's voice struck a chord, but I can't connect it to a face. I saw only legs while on the floor. The man kept to the background."

"Yeah, that's what I saw," Suzie said. "He wore black trousers. Black shoes. He kept out of sight, which tells me he was worried one of us might recognize him."

"We have your brothers in custody. Do you want to

press charges?" the policeman asked.

"Yes," Niall said without hesitation. "I got the impression they might be in the country illegally. I want Euan and Colin out of the UK. They should stay far away from me."

"Let us do our job," the policeman said, his eyes narrowing as he took in Niall's flinty expression. "Don't do anything silly."

Suzie rose and sidled closer to Niall. She placed her hand on his forearm in silent comfort. "Can we go home soon? It's been a harrowing day. I want to shower and retire."

"We have your statements and contact details," the policeman said. "Do you have someone to drop you home?"

"I'll call—" Niall started.

A voice hailed from down the passage. Scott.

"That sounds like my friend. He'll give us a ride home," Suzie said.

Neither she nor Niall spoke until they were traveling to the castle with Liam driving.

"I hope we did the right thing—getting the police involved," Scott said. "It was that or call Angus."

"You made the proper choice," Niall said. "My brothers deserve everything they have coming to them." He fell silent.

Suzie felt the tension quivering through his muscles. Her brother and sisters, although they were younger than her, would do anything to help her. They'd never knife her in the back, just as she'd never betray them. Did they argue? Sure. They were stubborn and liked to win, but they'd never hurt each other.

"Did you watch the building while waiting for the police to arrive?" Niall asked.

"Yes," Liam said. "I watched the front while Scott did the rear. No one approached or went inside."

"I didn't see anyone apart from one guy walking along the forest path that goes along the rear of the building. By the time I'd finished talking to the kids, he'd disappeared, so I think he was an innocent passerby," Scott said.

Suzie and Niall exchanged a knowing glance, their heads nodding in agreement.

"What was he wearing?" Suzie asked.

Scott glanced back at them from the passenger seat. His forehead creased. "Ah...dark clothes. Black sweater and trousers. I didn't see what color shoes he wore. Shortly after, the kids arrived and requested directions to the village. They were upset because they'd become lost and were late meeting their parents."

"The guy we heard with Euan and Colin wore black trousers. Did he have time to enter the building while you were talking to the kids?

"Hell," Scott said, his green eyes wide. "I'm sorry. The kids were so upset. I thought it was strange when they stopped crying so suddenly, but I decided it was relief at finding help. Yeah, he could've entered via the rear."

"I didn't see him leave through the front," Liam started, then rubbed a hand over his face, his expression turning to one of disgust. "An elderly lady drove past and stopped near me. She wound down her window and was crying. She told me she didn't drive often, and she'd taken a wrong turn. Her reaction was so plausible, even if she wasn't that lost. She simply had to turn around and return the same way. This guy used her as a distraction and left without me seeing."

"He was so careful to hide his face," Niall said.

"It has to be someone you know," Suzie said, studying Niall. With his battered face and rumpled appearance, he seemed older. The rougher edge suited him, but she wouldn't admit it. "I can't wait to jump into the shower. I feel as if I haven't been clean for days."

"What's our next step?" Scott asked.

Warmth filled Suzie, but she'd known her friends would want to help. They could see she was gone over Niall, even if he was standoffish today.

"You shouldn't get involved in this. You're heading home next week. Enjoy the last of the gathering before you leave," Niall said.

"We're Suzie's friends. You're her mate, which makes you our friend. We are offering our help. You need people around you who you can trust," Liam said with unfaltering logic.

"Besides, given this mystery man doesn't want his identity revealed, he's someone in your circle of acquaintances. More than ever, you need to surround yourself with friendly faces," Scott said, nailing Niall with a determined gaze. "You're stuck with us, buddy."

Niall's expression went slack for an instant, and Suzie would bet no one had offered him such unstinted aid before. Her heart hurt when she imagined the little boy he'd been. Frightened. Alone. Bullied by the people who should've acted as his support net. His transformation into a talented and driven person was truly wondrous. Her miracle man.

"Let Scott and Liam help. You can't trust everyone on your staff." Suzie paused, thinking. "Apart from Angus. He's loyal to you."

"What about business associates?" Scott asked. "That makes more sense, given they wanted your honey. You still need to write that list of your competitors and business associates."

Niall nodded. "Thank you for your offer of help. I hate to think someone close to me might be capable of this. No. I don't believe it."

Suzie opened her mouth to speak, but Liam beat her to it.

"Your honey is a big deal, and someone is actively trying to sabotage you. It's obvious they want your honey—probably to duplicate your efforts. You need to get past your loyalty to your staff and workers. If they're blameless, it means one of them has blabbed to a competitor, and that competitor wants to get his hands on your share of the honey market," Liam said.

"Or someone who helped to test your honey has spoken to someone they shouldn't have," Suzie said.

"It was a risk circulating the honey to testers, but I had to learn how good it was," Niall said. "I discovered it by accident, and I'm the only one who knows the hives' location and what the bees are feeding on to produce their honey. It was pure chance I noticed its unusual properties."

"Niall," Suzie said, "when someone broke into your premises, they didn't get the special honey. I thought you said that only you and your trusted assistant worked there plus Harris. Few knew this was your research and development hub. None of those who help to test your honey would know, which makes their involvement less likely. Where is your honey now?"

"Locked in the room next to mine at the castle," Niall said with satisfaction. "Only Angus knows it's there."

"Does Angus possess a room key?" Scott asked.

"I'd trust Angus with my life. He was my mentor's steward, and I've known him since I arrived in Scotland," Niall said stridently. "He's more of an advisor and a father figure than anything else."

"Does Angus resent you owning the castle?" Liam asked. "I assume your mentor left the property to you, or you purchased it from him."

"Angus and I own the castle jointly, although Angus hates to publicize that fact. My mentor left him lots of cash, and Angus owns a stake in my business. It wouldn't make sense for him to steal my honey or any proprietary information," Niall said. "Same goes for Harris. I've known him since my arrival, and Cameron left him a house by the coast. He also owns a small share of the honey business. Angus and Harris both pushed me to grow the business after Cameron died."

Suzie's brows rose on hearing this. "Why does Angus work as your steward if he doesn't need the money?"

"He likes to keep busy. It was his idea to have the gathering at the castle. He enjoys having younger people around the place," Niall said.

"All right," Scott said. "If Angus and Harris are clear, that leaves your assistant. Has your private investigator checked his background? The guy today kept out of sight."

"No, I can't believe... It has to be someone testing the honey for me," Niall said.

"You could find your brothers and ask them," Suzie suggested, her heart breaking for Niall. He refused to believe the increasingly plausible explanation.

19

BETRAYAL

B ONE-DEEP EXHAUSTION TUGGED AT Niall, every muscle and his head aching. How had it come to this? All he wanted was to market his honey and improve athletes' performances. It wasn't about money. He'd merely wanted to share the honey he'd discovered. His identification of its unique properties had happened by accident, and after he'd tested his theories, he realized he'd found a wonder product. The honey had made the difference, and he thought it might have other applications. What if it could help older people or those who were sick?

What should've been a happy and celebratory time had morphed into a nightmare.

Someone had ordered his brothers to kidnap Suzie, dragging her into this mess. He'd failed to keep her safe, and that fact taunted him.

Niall glanced in her direction and found her watching him. Her smile was soft and full of understanding he didn't deserve. That lush mouth of hers firmed, and she reached for his hand. She leaned against his arm, her scent filling his lungs. His bear gave a soft chuff of need, and Niall resettled, wrapping his arm around her and drawing her close.

"I'm sorry," he murmured.

"Why? None of this is your fault," Suzie said in surprise. "You didn't kidnap me. Your brothers are the problem. Will you hold Colin while I punch him in the nose?"

Niall spat out a laugh at her bloodthirsty query. "I could do that, but something tells me you can show my brothers your displeasure without my help."

Liam pulled up at the rear of the castle.

"Anyone hungry?" Niall asked. "Angus will want to whistle up breakfast for us. Feeding people is his way of dealing with a crisis."

"I could drink coffee," Suzie said. "I'm craving a shower."

Niall squeezed her gently. "You go and shower."

She blushed and leaned closer, whispering in his ear. "I was hoping you'd share with me."

"After I speak with Angus."

"I understand. He's your family," Suzie said. "I didn't see it before, but now I know you better, it's easy to see your bond. He's very proper in public, but I've heard him joke with you when you're alone."

"We're going to clean up," Scott said. "Why don't we meet for breakfast and a strategy meeting in an hour?"

"Works for me," Liam said.

Niall nodded and urged Suzie from the vehicle. "Go up while I speak with Angus."

The door to Niall's private entry flew open, and Angus filled the doorway. Once he spotted Niall, the anxiety in his thin face fell away. His assessing gaze took in the rest of them.

"You'll want coffee and something to eat," Angus said. "I'll speak with the cook."

"Can you deliver breakfast to the dining room in an hour?" Niall asked. "We want to shower and change clothes before we eat and devise a plan. Will you join us? We'd welcome your input."

Niall caught Angus's surprise, then the flash of pleasure that filled his narrow face. "I will be available."

Niall dipped his head in recognition. Liam and Scott disappeared, and Suzie hovered, waiting for him. His heart squeezed, and the gentle chuff from his bear urging him to touch her had him holding out his hand. She closed the distance between them, slipping her hand into his. Niall curled his fingers, his world righting despite the trouble surrounding them.

"Thank you," he said, tugging her from the entranceway toward the stairs leading to his private apartments.

"For what?"

"My brothers abducted you and kept you locked in a cold, drafty room. Even after your ordeal, you're calm. You're not blaming me for what my brothers did."

"Shouting won't help. Besides, I'm more pissed than upset. Your brothers are idiots. I don't have a high opinion

186

of the man pulling their strings, either. He's the one I blame for our trouble, and he's not brave enough to do his dirty work."

"True." A wealth of affection engulfed him. He wanted to hug her and snatch a kiss, but that could wait.

Niall hesitated outside his bedroom, needing to keep her close but not wanting to make assumptions.

"We can share a shower," Suzie said.

Her calm manner had his shoulders relaxing and his tension receding. Yet anger still crawled through his veins as he silently admitted his fear when he hadn't known where his brothers had taken her. Aware her gaze was turning quizzical, Niall nodded, not trusting himself to speak when fury pulsed through him.

He shouldered the door open, tugging her into his lair. He studied her face and scanned her to search for injuries, even though he'd done this earlier. "Are you all right?"

"A few bruises. Don't worry. I heal fast, just like you."

Suzie tugged away and stepped back to push off her shoes. Next came her clothes until she stood before him naked. Beautiful. Sleek curves and lots of tanned skin. A few freckles and definite bruises. Those he did not like, and he wished he'd bashed his brothers' heads together for the way they'd manhandled Suzie and inflicted pain on her.

"Niall?"

"You are so beautiful," Niall said, embarrassed at being caught staring.

"Hurry," she scolded. "Because I intend to use all of the hot water." She strode into the en suite, and his gaze followed, enjoying the sway of her backside. Seconds later, the shower started.

Niall grinned, suddenly lighthearted. He stripped, leaving his clothes where they fell because he was eager to join Suzie. Steam billowed when he entered the bathroom, and the citrus scent of his shower gel perfumed the air. His gaze shot to Suzie, standing beneath a shower head, her face tilted toward the water, and the last of his lingering tension faded.

His mate.

Niall stepped closer, not even flinching at the intense satisfaction emanating from his bear. He set his hands on her shoulder and drew her against his chest. His bear released a sigh, and Niall barely restrained his smile. This was what they both wanted. Suzie.

"I was frantic when you went missing," he said. "I need to strike against my brothers. They're determined to finish their sting and don't care who they hurt."

"If you paid them, they'd leave. For a while," she added. "They think they can grind you down. That's why they're doing their pain in the backside act. Could you get them deported? They're here illegally and have limited options."

"Apart from hiring an assassin to take me out," Niall said dryly. He slid his lips down the tender side of her neck and savored the tremble that ran through her. "I don't want to talk about my brothers. Not when I have my beautiful and sexy mate in my arms. Besides, we're on a tight schedule here. We're meeting the others for a meal."

Suzie turned in his arms, her smile sultry and enticing. She reached up to link her hands behind his neck and tugged down his head. "Let's not waste any more time."

Seconds later, her lips hit his.

Niall kissed her, savoring every nuance of the kiss—the press of lips against his, her peppermint taste, and the shy sweep of her tongue. Amazement and happiness flitted through him as he deepened the kiss and drew her closer, fitting her body to his. Despite a challenging life, he'd achieved his current position through hard work. He hadn't expected to find a mate, and he held and kissed her with a sense of wonderment.

Citrus filled his lungs, and clouds of steam heightened the sense of privacy and togetherness. This woman... She stole his breath. A partner in every sense of the word. She was perfect.

Niall eased back from the kiss and smiled at her swollen lips. His bear gave a chuff of approval but refrained from his usual litany.

"We should hurry," she reminded him.

"Aye," he said, "but I wish I'd suggested meeting for dinner so I could have you to myself for a few hours."

Her grin turned to a sultry smile that smoked his insides and had his body acting predictably. "We have tonight."

Niall grumbled but didn't honestly mind. He enjoyed every moment spent with Suzie. She was intelligent, relished business discussions, and liked the great outdoors. They fit together so well.

Suzie quickly washed her hair while Niall scrubbed away the dirt of the last twelve hours. While Suzie dried her hair, he dressed and pondered how to handle his brothers. After considering his options and the facts, he devised a plan.

He and Suzie arrived late to the dining room. Scott

and Liam were peppering Angus with questions about farming in Scotland, which Angus was knowledgeable about since he'd grown up on a farm and his family still raised Highland cattle.

"I like your friends. Shifters at the gathering mostly come from wealthy families. They're accustomed to servants, and they treat Angus like wallpaper."

Suzie glanced askance at him. "He stands for that?"

"They get the smaller rooms and slower service. He does this so skillfully they don't realize the slight." Niall grinned. "You and your friends scored some of the nicer rooms."

Suzie sniffed. "We're also scoring a delicious breakfast. I smell bacon and tattie scones." She patted her butt. "Angus's breakfasts have added to my padding."

Niall ran his hand down her back and cupped her rear. He squeezed. "Nothing wrong with your backside," he whispered. "I like it very much."

Scott glanced up from his heaped plate and rolled his eyes. "*Eww!* Enough of that. It reminds me that I haven't found a mate and, therefore, are game for the single shifters. Those shifter women scare me."

"Some males have intense focus, too. I heard there was a big fight last night when three male shifters paid attention to one female. Angus told us they had to call in security to deal with the fallout," Liam said.

"Hell," Niall said. An understatement. That wasn't what he and Angus had intended when devising the gathering.

"A lot of it is pressure from home," Suzie said.

"Consider having everyone sign a waiver. Primarily, this gathering is for networking, and those who haven't found mates shouldn't feel like failures."

"Agreed," Angus said, placing a carafe of coffee on the table.

"It's an expense to some who desperately require fresh blood in their packs or clans." Niall frowned, considering the options. "I wonder if those who don't find mates could receive a discounted rate. We can interview them to gain insight into their failure."

"I wouldn't call it a failure. Some have other goals and don't want a mate," Scott said. "Saber and London made it clear we shouldn't feel pressure to find a mate. The gathering was to meet other shifters our age and make contacts that might benefit us and our town. We've learned from speaking with other shifters that most alphas expected their people to return home with mates. That's what upped the tension this week."

"Yep," Liam said before shoving half a rasher of bacon into his mouth.

"They're right," Suzie said.

Niall pulled out a chair for Suzie and seated her. He hadn't been looking for a mate, hadn't thought he deserved one, but Suzie fit seamlessly into his life. He dropped into the seat beside her and accepted the coffee she poured him with a smile of thanks.

"I may attend this afternoon and deliver a speech. How many single shifters are left?"

Angus hovered near the doorway. "Two hundred and forty-eight," he said.

191

"Have you eaten breakfast?" Suzie asked him.

"Yes," Angus said.

"Sit with us and have a coffee or a cup of tea," she said. "Your hovering is making me nervous."

Niall hid his amusement by sipping his coffee while Angus did as Suzie bid. Scott asked Angus a question before he became too self-conscious.

"Tea, please."

Suzie shunted a cup in Angus's direction. "The tea is closer to you. You sure you don't want a tattie scone? They're delicious. I need the recipe before I go home."

The casual words sent a dart through Niall's gut, the shock of it stealing his breath. Suzie was going home? They hadn't discussed her departure, but he'd assumed...

Niall shook away his panic, the haze disappearing entirely with a sharp kick to his calf. He jerked his head up to meet Angus's glare.

Niall cleared his throat. Angus was right, even though it wasn't his desired topic. "Suzie, I'd hoped you'd forgiven my stupidity and would stay with me. We haven't had time to discuss the future yet, but we're mates. We belong together." His heart pounded louder than usual as he waited for her reply. Even his bear remained silent, the torturous delay wearing on both.

Suzie smiled, the curve of her lips transforming her face into mesmerizing. So beautiful. *His.*

"I'm going home briefly to see my family and report to Saber and London. I also need to contact the university and sort that out. Maybe you could come with me."

Relief was a heady balm, and Nial slumped

momentarily before he grinned at his mate in return. "I'd love that. While I travel to Europe and Scandinavia regularly, I haven't visited your region before."

Liam rolled his eyes. "Now that's settled, what's our plan? Who do we think is responsible?"

Niall filled the details in for Angus, and the elderly shifter picked up his mug of tea, his piercing eyes shining with disappointment. Niall felt the same disillusion lodged in his belly.

"Ah, Angus and I are of one accord." Niall sighed, aware he did so to stall. The pain was like a knife, worsened by the knowledge that his family would swindle him if he gave them a chance. "The only person with the same in-depth information about the new honey is Michael, who runs the bottling plant. He has access to my research premises and other inside information. Harris has inside knowledge, but he's close to Angus. Besides, every second week, he visits his daughter in Edinburgh. He hasn't been here to create mischief."

"He could've paid someone," Liam said.

"Aye, that's true, but I can't see it. Besides, he has had access to the honey the entire time." No, Angus was right. Harris would never betray either of them.

"Where do you bottle—is that the right word?" Scott asked. "Your manufacturing premises. Where is that?"

"I planned to do a limited run and operate the process myself. I produced the samples, and the idea was to restrict the supply since I only have a few hives."

"Does this Michael know the hives' location?" Liam asked.

"No, although he asks me all the time. It has become an inside joke between us." A sick sensation swirled through Niall's belly, leaving him no longer hungry. He tried to wash away the horrid taste with a swallow of coffee. "After the break-in at the research premises, I brought everything back here. Michael doesn't have access."

"What about the samples?" Suzie asked.

"All tightly controlled and already consumed. It was a side project for me, and Michael had less input than usual."

"Apart from the results," Angus said. "He helped you collate those and wasn't that when your problems started? You had issues in the factory, minor things you handled and didn't think much of. In retrospect, the small issues have become significant."

"Yes," Niall said, agreeing. Accepting the brutal betrayal was hard despite its obviousness.

"We know who and how, but how can we prove it?" Suzie asked.

"Give him enough rope to hang himself," Angus said with a predatory grin. "We set him up and take him down."

Liam bit off a piece of toast, chewed, and swallowed it. "I like the way you think. Can we set it up for the weekend? That gives us two days."

Niall wanted this over, but they couldn't hurry and scare Michael off. "You're right. Although I am inclined to confront him, catching him in the act would be more satisfying."

"Are we positive this assistant is your culprit?" Liam

asked.

"We'll set a honey trap," Angus announced. "To part innocent from guilty."

20

MESSAGE FROM HOME

SUZIE GIGGLED WHILE PREPARING for bed. "A honey trap?"

Niall paused, unbuttoning his shirt, his face impassive, but Suzie was starting to understand this somber bear. A glint shone in his eyes, and she knew he understood the joke and was pretending otherwise.

His brows quirked. "What else would you call it?"

"Angus lightening the mood," she said, still grinning. "He's usually serious and stern. I was a little scared of him when we first arrived."

"He takes pride in his job. He doesn't need to work but does it because he says the contact with the shifters keeps him young."

"Angus is scary efficient."

"I'll tell you a secret," Niall said, his fingers at his belt buckle now.

"What?" Suzie's gaze followed his hand with interest. The intimacy was new but right for her. Now that she'd met Niall and her plans had changed, she understood Edwina's actions. When a mate came along, one's choices changed. The goalposts shifted with different priorities.

"Angus scared me at first, too."

Suzie laughed and reached for a sleep T-shirt before hesitating. Dressing was a wasted effort. Niall always slept naked, and she wanted to feel skin against skin.

"Where have your thoughts gone?"

"I was thinking about sleep and nakedness and deciding not to bother dressing for bed."

"Great minds think alike." Niall slid out of his black trousers and underwear. He winked at her before dropping his clothing over the back of an upright chair and padding across the thick woolen carpet to the king-size bed.

Suzie watched his tight butt and barely withheld her sigh of appreciation. He was a huge man with defined muscles. It was no hardship to watch him flex that sexy physique. It was almost as good as touching.

Aware she was wasting time, Suzie undressed and set her discarded clothes beside Niall's. She could feel him watching her, appreciating her body and tried hard not to blush.

Niall pulled her into his arms, and she breathed in his honied scent. He always smelled so decadent and enticing.

"How are you feeling after my brothers manhandled you?" he asked. "We've been discussing our plan and suspicions, but I should've been cossetting you instead."

Suzie kissed his cheek, savoring the slight abrasion of whiskers. She slipped her arms around his neck. "A few bumps and bruises, but they're not too bad. My shifter side has mostly healed my ouchies."

"I'm sorry it happened. It's all my fault."

"Rubbish. The problem lies with your brothers and the person at the top. Even though I laughed at your honey trap, it's the perfect idea to flush out the leader. If he wants your honey so much, let him think he has it. What did the investigator say?"

"I haven't caught up with him yet. He was busy when I rang a few minutes ago."

"Okay. Enough of this discussion. Let's come up with more enjoyable activities."

Niall nuzzled her cheek. "Do tell."

Suzie stretched up on tiptoes and wound her arms around his neck. She grinned, and seconds later, he covered her mouth with his, kissing her until her knees went weak and her head spun. She felt weightless and opened her eyes to find Niall had scooped her up. He placed her on the bed and followed her down. His smile was wide and flirtatious, his expression reminding her of a marauding pirate.

"Sir, now that you have me in your clutches, whatever shall I do?"

Niall rolled his eyes. "Do I have to spell it out, lass?"

"Yes," Suzie said, and a bubble of laughter filled her, aching for freedom. She'd never thought of fun and laughter in conjunction with making love. She loved seeing Niall's playful side.

"I'm a lucky man." Niall kissed the side of her neck.

"You smell good."

"It's your shower gel."

"Yes," he said with quiet satisfaction. "I thought having a woman in my life would change everything. It has, but I like the differences. I enjoy having you here to discuss my honey, the gathering, or the weather. My life was lacking before you came along."

Suzie laughed, her green eyes twinkling. "You've changed everything for me as well." She initiated a kiss, and intense yearning crawled through her. Although sex was new to her, she wanted to touch him and receive touches in return. As if he could read her mind, his hips pressed into hers, and he took over the kiss. He nibbled and licked until she gasped and dragged him even closer, surrendering to his greater experience.

She ran her hands over his shoulders, her nails digging into his flesh. Niall's mouth shifted into a smile, or at least, it felt that way. When she opened her eyes to look, she found she was right. She wriggled and moved her hips against him, her breath hitching at the bulge of his cock. She wriggled again and laughed at the growl that emerged from him. Niall sucked lightly on the skin of her neck. It was enough for her to feel the suction but not enough to bruise for everyone to see later.

Meanwhile, Suzie made free with Niall's body, touching everywhere she could reach. Her hand smoothed over his butt and lingered. Now that he was naked, it was much easier to appreciate his splendor.

"You keep drifting off," he murmured against her breasts.

"Nope. Merely thinking about your biteable muscles and how much I'd like to see my teeth marks on your butt."

Niall blinked, and she glimpsed his bear in his eyes. Suzie laughed, a bark of hilarity that sounded more like a cackle. But heck, Niall's bear was totally on board with biting and the resulting badges of honor.

Niall stared at her, blinking several more times, his manner uncharacteristically diffident. Suzie laughed again and was still laughing when her cell phone rang. She jumped at the burst of familiar music—the upbeat tune about family telling her it was a call from home. One she wasn't expecting. Tension slid through her, canceling her merriment. She wrenched from Niall's embrace and groped for her phone.

"Suzie?" The surprise in his voice told her he didn't understand why she wouldn't let the caller leave a message. It was late now—close to midnight. The ringing continued, becoming more insistent, and panic rose in her. Where the devil was her phone? She ran her hand over the bedside cabinet and finally, finally she located it. The phone thumped to the floor, and she scrambled after it. A tremble darted through her, settling in her fingers and making her fumble as she attempted to answer the call. "Dad? Mum?"

Instead, it was Charlie, her brother, the sibling closest to her age. "Suzie?" His voice wasn't more than a whisper.

"What's wrong?" Her breath burst in and out, audible to her and probably to Niall. She shot a glance at him. He wore a scowl, and she jerked, shocked at this reaction.

"Mum and Dad were in an accident. Gran told me not

200

to ring," he blurted.

"You've done the right thing," she reassured him, hearing the quiver in his voice. "Mum and Dad—"

"Dad has bad bruises. Mum is worse. She's still unconscious."

Suzie heard the unshed tears. The shock. Her family needed her. "I'll catch the first flight home."

"I'm sorry, Suzie," Charlie said.

"Don't be silly. Give me progress reports via email or text. You mightn't be able to contact me while I'm on the flight, but I'll call you before I board the plane."

"Thanks, Suzie." An audible swallow sounded. "We're scared."

"Where's Gran?" Suzie asked.

"She's gone on holiday to Wellington with Grandpa."

Ah. Well, she couldn't blame her grandparents. They'd been discussing their holiday for months and had saved to stay at a spa hotel.

"What does Gavin say?" Gavin was the shifter community doctor. If the accident had been local, Gavin would've treated her parents.

"He says they'll be okay. They're banged up, and Mum will wake soon. The truck hit on the passenger side, but Mum will be okay because she is a shifter."

Okay. Despite the good news, her desire to go home remained. "Who is staying with you?"

"No one."

Anger burned away her fear. Had anyone considered her siblings? They shouldn't be alone.

"Someone is here," Charlie said, his voice squeaking

with alarm. "Should I answer the door?"

Suzie closed her eyes. "Approach the door and sniff to identify the person outside. I'll be here while you check."

"Okay," Charlie said.

When she heard his feet stomping on the floor, she couldn't help but smile. Despite his feline nature, Charlie was a typical boy who went nowhere quietly unless he was in his leopard form.

"It's Mr. Saber," Charlie said. "Should I let him inside?"

The release of tension had her knees quivering, and she sank onto the edge of the mattress. "Yes, ask him if I can speak to him."

The door creaked, and a sweet ache pierced her heart as she thought of a breakfast table discussion before she left for Scotland. Her mother had been after her dad to oil the hinges. That obviously hadn't happened yet.

"Suzie," came the familiar voice.

"Saber, have you heard how Mum and Dad are?"

"I've come from Gavin's surgery. Your mum has regained consciousness, but she has a dislocated shoulder and a broken leg. Your father has bruising around his chest from the seat belt. They're confused, but Gavin says they'll recover."

"Thank goodness. I'll get a flight home as soon as I can."

"London and I talked and thought you'd want to do that. London has arranged a flight home for you. Just show up at the airport. She's emailing the details to you. I told her I'd call you."

"Thank you, Saber."

"No problem," Saber said in his easy way. "Since your

grandparents are away, I'll stay with your brother and sisters tonight. If Gavin wants to keep your mother in for another day, London and I will handle your siblings."

"Thanks. I appreciate it."

"Not a problem." Saber laughed. "My daughters are hosting two friends for a sleepover. It is more peaceful in your house."

"I wouldn't count on it," Suzie said, knowing that Saber loved his twin girls and would do anything for his family.

"I'll see you soon. Sorry you're cutting your holiday short. If you need anything, contact London or me, okay?"

"I will. Thanks again." Suzie hung up and blinked hard. Her parents would be okay, and Saber was with her siblings. She brushed the moistness from her eyes and stood. The majority of her possessions were still in the room she'd used for the gathering. She hurriedly grabbed her clothes and started dressing.

"What are you doing?" Niall asked. His words were cool, with little expression.

"I'm going to pack. My family needs me."

"But you were going to help me," Niall said.

Suzie froze, not liking his defensive and slightly surly tone. Surely, he must understand she had to leave. It wasn't as if he couldn't cope without her. "I'm sorry, but I must go. You have a plan. It's a solid one, and I'm positive you'll catch your honey thief."

Suzie finished dressing and scanned the room for any other possessions. Ah, her shopping. She scooped up the bags and turned to Niall. "I'm sorry, but I have to leave."

"Fine," Niall said, sitting on the edge of the bed now, his

large body taut with tension.

Suzie hesitated, wanting to go to him, kiss him goodbye, and wish him good luck. But Niall radiated anger and impatience, so she kept her distance. "Bye, Niall."

He didn't reply, and she blinked hard to hold back the burn of tears. Right then. A blast of anger propelled her to the door. He was acting like a petulant child—just like he had earlier when he'd jumped to conclusions. Where was the trust? The understanding? Her family needed her at home, and she wanted to support them. It wasn't her fault Niall allowed his childhood to color his reactions. She lifted her chin, allowing herself one last look at the man who'd come to mean everything to her. It was apparent he didn't feel quite the same way, and it hurt, damn it.

Suzie dragged her gaze away and yanked the door open. Her steps were jerky as she walked away, and maintaining composure was one of the toughest challenges she had ever faced.

The snick of the door closing behind her was a final blow because she hadn't closed it.

Niall had.

21

I'M AN IDIOT

"WHERE'S SUZIE?" LIAM ASKED as he and Scott arrived in the breakfast room. A silent Angus strode after them with a fresh pot of coffee.

Niall grunted and continued eating his breakfast. She'd left him. His bear released an unhappy chuff, the dejected sound audible. He spotted the look Liam and Scott exchanged, and that irritated him. She'd left him, and it shouldn't be a surprise.

His bear emitted a pitiful moan next. Niall clenched his knife and fork harder and kept devouring his breakfast, even though he was no longer hungry. Or happy. His gut was already telling him he'd screwed up spectacularly.

Angus murmured something to Liam and Scott, no doubt telling them that Suzie had gone home.

Liam slipped into the chair beside Niall while Scott took the one opposite.

"Suzie is close to her family," Liam said. "She's the oldest, and her siblings look up to her. Are her parents going to be okay?"

"She told me the prognosis was good for both parents, but she felt that they and her brother and sisters required her support," Angus said from where he hovered at the doorway. His expression was full of disapproval and disappointment.

"She left me," Niall snapped, his anger aimed more at himself now. His lack of empathy hadn't helped. He hadn't behaved like a friend or a mate, dammit. *Aw, hell.* He glanced up to see judgment and censure, an attitude he deserved.

Scott goggled at him, his mouth dropping open. "Her family needed her. Suzie has a big heart. Of course, she'd go home early."

Liam scowled at him. "Suzie loves you, you great big dunderhead."

"Niall thinks all families are traitorous and after everything they can get," Angus said, nailing Niall with a glare. "He doesn't understand not all are like his. Love and care are common in most families."

"Suzie is your mate," Scott said. "Of course, she cares for you, but you put her in an awkward situation. You demanded she stay and forced her to choose."

Liam reached for a piece of toast. "Scott, don't be too hard on Niall. You have a decent family who care for you. Not everyone has families like you and Suzie. Mine treat me like crap and screw with my head. Jerk with my emotions. His brothers have been messing with him. It's no wonder he's not thinking straight." Liam focused on Niall. "Don't be an idiot and let Suzie leave. She's worth fighting for. Think of it this way. With Suzie, you get a mate with an enormous heart. You have her loyalty, and she'd bite off her hand rather than hurt you. Not only do you win Suzie, but you gain a family and a large circle of friends. You'll have found a family who'll welcome you because you're with Suzie."

Scott nodded. "We should wrap up your problem with your honey and return to Middlemarch together. You come with us, go to Suzie, and beg her forgiveness. Honestly, if you don't, you're dumber than I thought. This mistake is fixable, but you should buy her a present and grovel big time."

"Suzie is worth the effort," Angus added, his tone full of approval for her while he glowered at Niall.

Mine! Mine! Mine!

"Thanks." Niall set his knife and fork across the middle of his plate and tried to block out his bear. He was only partially successful. He'd try to call Suzie. Apologize.

"One more thing," Scott said. "Suzie, Liam, and I arrived with three additional friends. I didn't know them well before, but this experience has brought us closer. Our entire community is like a big family; if you and Suzie end up together, you'll become part of it. Middlemarch is an amazing place. My cousin Saber is in charge and supports those in his community. I bet he or London has already sorted out help for Suzie's parents and looking after her brother and sisters. Your family doesn't define you; there are people who care. Those people are your family, and you give and hold to them in return. They are your team. Look, Suzie cares for you. Her scent wouldn't cling to you otherwise. With her at your side, you'll have a big-ass family who have your back. Blood might not connect you, but they'll be encouraging and loyal and sometimes pains in the arse. Don't chuck this opportunity away because of hurt pride or rotten memories."

"Couldn't have said it better," Liam exclaimed, raising his hand for a high five.

Scott beamed as he slapped his friend's palm.

Angus met Niall's gaze and gave an imperceptible nod, lifting some of the weight on Niall's shoulders.

"I'll think about what you've said," he promised. He had dated women previously, always being the one to end things. He'd never experienced this sense of emptiness. Yet Scott and Liam were correct. Suzie had intended to go home next week. He hadn't asked her to stay. He'd commanded her rather than asking properly. He'd given her sweet words, but he hadn't claimed her because, deep down, he was still that scared child trying to protect his heart. He needed to woo her instead of taking her for granted. Basically, what Angus had told him during his lecture before he'd handed over breakfast.

"Let's go over our plan again," he said, finding the shift of topic eased his tension. In his business realm, he exuded confidence and knew precisely how to proceed. Romance and love were beyond his ken, but he'd get there. Eventually.

Tension simmered through Niall as he settled in his tiny

office, but he quashed the emotion, determined to act naturally and flush out his honey thief. Liam and Scott had hidden inside the nearby research building, their feline senses allowing them to perceive others easily. They were his backup, and he was grateful for their unstinting support.

Angus remained at the castle, a phone call away.

Confidence in their plan cut away at his anxiety. It was an excellent strategy, and damn if he'd let someone else steal his honey. Let them work to produce their own miracle.

The purr of a motor vehicle pulling up outside had him straightening. *Showtime*. His bear's chuff echoed in his mind, leading Niall to a decision.

They were right. Angus, too. He loved Suzie, and she made him happy. He didn't know why, but his ray of sunshine had embraced his grumpiness. Because of Suzie, he had two new friends at his back. Afterward, he planned to fly to New Zealand. He'd beg for forgiveness and tell Suzie he loved her and couldn't live without her. She'd supported him fully with his honey, but he hadn't given her the same level of backing with her music. That changed now.

His bear gave a testy chuff, and Niall grinned. Aye, they'd claim their woman and love her until none of them doubted where they stood.

The car door slammed, and Niall forced his thoughts to the present. Rapid footsteps came closer, and the door squeaked as a hand yanked it open.

"Niall, I didn't expect you here. I thought you were

working from the castle," Michael said. He was a height-challenged man, but his suit and crisp cotton shirt gave him an elegant air. His brown eyes were shrewd and full of confidence. Right now, they held a trace of alarm.

Niall needed to nullify Michael's suspicions. "I had a folder of research notes here. In the turmoil after the break-in, I missed grabbing it. I was just about to tidy up and search for my folder. How is the advertising campaign going?"

"We've hit a few snags. I was going to call you after I checked through everything again."

Niall glanced at his watch. "I have a meeting but can return this afternoon." Niall met Michael's gaze and took satisfaction in the fact that Michael glanced away first, under the excuse of checking his diary.

"I have a marketing meeting at midday. Could we meet later in the afternoon? Around four?"

Niall considered their plan. "Could you make it four-thirty? That would give me leeway if my three o'clock meeting goes long."

"I'll be here. I'll leave you to it and go over the marketing plan. Hopefully, I have time to tidy a bit before leaving."

"Thanks," Niall said, working hard to keep his voice even. He didn't want to scare the man off. Every sign pointed to Michael's perfidy, and Niall wanted to learn how deep the rot ran. Did Michael have others working with him, or was he the boss? The brains behind this attempted heist? "I'll see you later." He glanced at his watch. "Damn, I'd better go, or I'll be late. We'll discuss the marketing budget and hash out any problems this afternoon."

Michael gave a quick nod before disappearing into the area where he worked. Niall glared after him. He'd checked the marketing budget a few days ago. All their ducks were in a row, and they had done nothing unusual that might cause problems. They'd decided on a low-key plan because they would never have a vast stock of honey. Niall hoped word of mouth would kick in and he'd amass loyal customers.

The next problem: he'd need to replace Michael with someone he could trust. That might take more work and research. Angus might have some ideas.

Anger filled Niall as he picked up his phone and the papers he'd been pretending to work on when Michael came to see him. It galled him he couldn't just punch the man, but there was a chance Michael wasn't responsible, and someone else was after his honey. He had to be certain. Also, deep in his gut, he knew Suzie would want him to behave to plan rather than using his fists. He aimed to be the man Suzie admired and loved and not act like his brothers.

Without hesitation, he rose and departed his research building, not bothering to check for Scott or Liam. It was one of the hardest things he'd ever done.

Until he came to Scotland, he had only himself to count on. Everything changed when the laird and Angus entered his life. Now, he was taking another step and letting in Suzie's friends—still a challenge for him but necessary.

He didn't want to remain a loner. He wanted Suzie and everything a relationship with her might encapsulate.

Niall left the research building and drove to a stand of pine trees. Liam and Scott would contact him as soon as something happened. He called Angus to give him an update.

"What does your gut say?" Angus asked after Niall had explained what had happened.

"I think Michael is our thief. I don't know whether it's greed or another reason, but I wish he'd talked to me."

"And said what?" Angus said. "You're the boss, the brainchild behind the honey. You've paid him well for his work. Why should he claim anything more from you?"

"You're right," Niall said after a pause.

"Keep me posted," Angus said. "I need to deal with a supplier who neglected to deliver half of my order."

The phone clattered, and Niall grinned, affection for the brusque elderly man filling him. Suzie came to mind, and the warmth morphed into something deeper. He loved the woman. Soon, he promised himself. Soon, he'd see Suzie again and tell her.

Niall's phone vibrated, and he scooped it off the passenger seat to check the screen. "Scott," he said. "What's happening?"

"He found the honey and the paperwork and made a phone call to someone called Timothy. He's en route and will arrive shortly. Liam and I will follow on foot."

"See you soon." Niall disconnected and shoved the phone in his pocket. After a brief pause, he pulled it back out and set his voice recorder app going. Michael wouldn't expect him, and hopefully, nervousness or arrogance would get the man talking. If he could record the conversation, Michael couldn't deny everything later. Niall strode onto the narrow gravel road and planted his feet in the middle. Michael might panic and try to run him over, but Niall didn't think his employee had it in him.

Niall heard the vehicle before he saw it, and he took great satisfaction in observing Michael's shock. His face turned pale, and the car kicked up dust and bits of gravel as he tried to evade Niall and drive around him. Niall leaped in front of the vehicle, and Michael automatically slammed on the brakes.

Liam and Scott appeared behind Michael's vehicle, and Niall saw when Michael realized they had him surrounded. He wound down his window. "What the devil are you doing? I thought you had a meeting."

"That's what you were meant to think. Do you have my honey?"

Michael's mouth opened and closed, fishlike, while his gaze shifted left and right. Niall went on the attack.

"Who is Timothy?"

Michael hesitated before blurting, "One of my marketing contacts."

"Oh? Not Timothy Campbell, the head of Heather Mountain Honey? Not Timothy, my major competitor?"

Michael did his fish impression again, his bulging eyes adding an extra element. "No, Timothy is the new marketing head at the agency."

"So if I search your vehicle, I won't find my notes folder or the labeled jars of honey I hid in the back of my office cupboard?" Niall asked, maintaining eye contact the entire time. Icy anger pulsed through his veins, fury at Michael's treacherous acts, and a profound disappointment in himself because he'd trusted the man. His mind wandered over the betrayals he'd suffered in the past, the swift kicks to his gut inflicted by his family and others. "Michael?"

Michael's shoulders slumped briefly before straightening, and his face contorted into rage. His eyes grew wide, the whites showing. His nostrils flared, and he took half a step toward Niall. "You know nothing." His finger jabbed at Niall, and he would've made contact if Niall hadn't stepped back. "I've worked for the laird since I left university. Each day I worked damn hard, and then he gave everything to an uneducated hick from the colonies. He owed me, dammit."

"This is about money?" Niall asked, stupidly feeling surprised along with his shock. The laird had left Michael a handsome legacy.

"The laird promised he'd look after me. He promised." Spittle flew with his vehemence, and a blood vessel throbbed at his temple.

"But he left you an inheritance."

Red raced over Michael's face, leaving his skin mottled and flushed. His fists clenched. Unclenched. Clenched. "I deserved more. He gave you everything."

Niall hadn't expected the gift, and he'd wanted to reject it until Angus had talked to him and told him the laird saw himself in Niall. Cameron Glenkirk had given Niall a chance, and Niall had worked hard, never disappointing the elderly man. Angus had told Niall he'd gifted the old man happiness and joy, and he thought of Niall as an adopted son. Niall and Cameron had strolled the estate, both enjoying the outdoors. He'd shared his bear shifter, and the laird had been thrilled, laughing with delight and telling Niall that was why he was so gifted with honey.

The laird had liked Michael, but they hadn't shared the same love and passion for nature. Angus had explained to Niall why the laird left him part of the estate. Michael would've sold everything. Niall sensed this truth deep in his gut. Michael wouldn't have kept and nurtured the wilderness. That didn't make him an evil man, but he hadn't shared the laird's vision. That had made the difference.

Niall mentioned none of this, and looking at Michael now, a swell of pity engulfed him. "If you needed money, why didn't you ask me for a loan?"

"A loan?" Michael scoffed. "You expect me to come to you, cap in hand, and ask for money?"

"I thought we were friends," Niall said. One of a small group.

"Friends!" Michael's disgusted snort told Niall everything.

The man had shown him a deceptive face.

"What do you want?" Niall said.

"I want everything. The estate. The money and all the castle's contents. I deserve that, at least."

"No." Niall refused to let Michael destroy the laird's legacy.

"Then I'll take your honey," Michael said. "I deserve something for the years I've labored to make the money the laird gave you."

"Take it," Niall said. "But know this. If you step foot on my property again, I will have you arrested. You kidnapped my girlfriend and hounded me. You destroyed my property and dragged my brothers into this entire mess."

Michael snickered. "Yeah, and it was funny as hell watching you chasing your tail, trying to figure out what was happening. I heard the girl ran home. Too bad." He sneered.

"You wanted my honey all along, and you didn't care what you did or who you hurt to get it," Niall snapped. *Admit it, you bastard. Admit it so I have everything recorded.*

"What's wrong with that?" Michael said.

"If you don't know the answer, then I'm wasting my time. You're a kidnapper and a thief. Take my honey and leave. But remember this: if I catch you on my property again, I *will* call the cops and press charges." Niall stepped away from Michael's vehicle but didn't make the mistake of turning his back. He didn't trust the man. The second Michael discovered the honey he'd stolen was a plain clover blend honey purchased from the supermarket, he'd be dangerous.

Niall watched Michael speed away, the vehicle fishtailing on the gravel before straightening. Michael wouldn't get away with his skullduggery. Niall would make sure of it. He picked up his phone to call his shifter contact on the local police force.

22

MISSING

"LET'S GO FOR A run," Scott said almost two hours later.

Niall ceased his pacing by his office desk, his head jerking up to stare at Scott. He slipped his phone into his pocket after leaving yet another message for Suzie. He'd really screwed up this time. His brows drew together, echoing the shock that still rippled through him at the suggestion. "You want to run with me?"

"Great idea," Liam said. "We're all edgy as hell, waiting to hear from the cops. I'm sure Angus will field the call for us when it comes."

"But I'm a bear," Niall said.

"So?" Scott said.

"I always run alone. Bears don't mass with other shifters."

"You're our friend. Since Suzie likes you, we've adopted

you. When you fly back with us to New Zealand, you'll see what it's like at home. Middlemarch is a multi-cultural town. We have humans, of course, but we're predominantly a community of black leopard shifters with a snow leopard and a spotted leopard for variety. Also wolves, tigers, and lions. We have human/shifter pairings. The Feline Council is supportive of every shifter in our town. We haven't had a bear before, but it won't matter. You're our friend. You're Suzie's mate. Everyone will accept you," Liam said. "Scott and I are newcomers, and everyone has made us welcome. You'll see."

Scott nodded. "He's right. Saber doesn't stand for any crap. He's married to a human, and Emily is amazing. Everyone loves her."

"Besides, we don't know the best places to run. Please show us some of your estate. What we've seen so far is stunning."

Niall grinned while praying that Suzie would give him another chance. "I still pinch myself some days that I own this land." Not a twinge of guilt came to him when he uttered these words, despite Michael's insulting assertions. His implication Niall had tricked the laird into leaving him the castle and the surrounding estate was ridiculous.

Niall had nothing to prove. Instead, he needed to live his best life, and that was one with Suzie—if she'd forgive him and offer a second chance.

"Let me talk to Angus and tell him where we're going," Niall said. "We can run up to the highest point. It's out of bounds to the gathering, so we won't run into anyone else."

"Can we shift here? Or do we need to hike into the forest?" Scott asked, his eyes bright with eagerness.

"We'll shift in the room off the kitchen. Angus will let us into the garden," Niall said.

Five minutes later, they burst into the fresh air. Niall led the way, loping past the rose garden, memories of the laird filling him as he took in the sweet fragrance. The old laird had loved his plants and flowers, and Niall had walked with him here every evening.

A ritual of sorts. One that he enjoyed. Back then, Michael had scoffed and pushed away the laird's invitations to join them. Walking outdoors had been no hardship to Niall. It had calmed his bear. He and Cameron had spoken of nothing important most times. Sometimes, the laird had told him stories about his childhood with his sister.

The old man hadn't been stupid, just lonely. With added years, Niall saw this clearly.

Niall breathed in the rose-scented air, suddenly at peace. Even his family didn't pain him as much in this moment. Maybe he'd search out his brothers before he left for New Zealand. They'd leave empty-handed because he'd ensure they understood he would never give them money. Seeing them would help with closure.

When he found the two black leopards were keeping up without difficulty, he increased his speed. They burst into the wildness of the forest, the scent of pine and beech trees exhilarating after being inside. Each of his senses was sharper, and he could hear the small forest creatures—the squirrels and birds. The breeze ruffled his fur, and he ran even faster, enjoying the bunch of his muscles. At the crest of the hill, he halted to study the castle in the valley below. The loch glinted in the sunlight, a jewel surrounded by massive trees.

Scott and Liam stopped beside him, their long tails waving behind them. Two black leopards, and they were his friends, despite their brief acquaintance. Niall felt quiet acceptance and gratitude. Contentment. His life was about to alter, but Angus believed change was beneficial. In the past, he'd grunted agreement when he preferred the status quo.

Now, at the top of this mountain, understanding filled him.

His honey business wasn't urgent. The recipe remained safe from potential robbers. Suzie had become vital to him, and it was time to quit protecting himself and step forward confidently. He needed to prove to Suzie he deserved her.

Everything else could wait.

They hadn't discussed where they would live. Scotland was his home, but she was close to her family. He didn't mind traveling, but Angus always told him he was working too hard.

He'd take time off.

Niall released a chuff, and Scott and Liam glanced askance at him. He couldn't speak now but would later at the castle. Right now, he was hot and wanted a swim. Niall trotted away and glanced over his shoulder to check if the black leopards were following. They were, without hesitation, and that warmed him. Contentment spread through him again.

He upped the pace until he loped along the forest paths, taking in the scents and sights in one long stream of information. The enticing aroma of honey almost drew him to a stop. An undiscovered wild hive. He slowed, but no, this was time for play. The hive would stay until he was ready to investigate. Niall kept up his hustle until he scented water.

The waterfall's source was higher in the hills and icy cold, but his thick fur kept him warm. He reached the path's edge, the pool at the bottom of the fall before him. He paused briefly, scanning for new debris, before leaping with a mighty splash.

Either way, these kitties would get wet.

He chuckled at the growl of displeasure but kept swimming, his powerful paws dragging him through the current. When he turned, he witnessed the two leopards leaping. As one, they struck the water. Twin roars had Niall chuffing and grunting in amusement, the joyous sound unusual enough to make him start. Friends. It was wonderful to have friends.

"You could've warned us the water was that cold," Scott grumbled half an hour later back at the castle. "My balls drew up so high, I doubt they'll come back soon. Just as well I haven't found a mate with sexual expectations."

Liam chuckled. "Well played, bear. But you should watch your back when you visit Middlemarch. I hear payback is a bitch."

Niall lifted his whisky glass in a silent toast, wanting to laugh but not quite daring. "You don't mind me flying back with you?"

"Our flight is next Tuesday," Scott said. "Liam and I have a brief stopover in Dubai before grabbing the next leg of our flight. We decided we didn't want to mess around with a stopover. We're ready to get back to our routine."

Niall listened to Liam and Scott describe the farms they worked on and the duties they performed with interest. "Maybe I can visit your farms while I'm in Middlemarch. The laird never had much domestic stock."

"Sure," Liam said, winking at Scott. "We can push him into a muddy puddle or get him to help clean the pigsty."

"We've got the last grand dinner, and then we'll be packing to head home," Scott said. "Could you join us for dinner? You can act as our wingman."

"I could do that," Niall said. "I'm meant to do a speech. If you want, I can have Angus switch the seating so you're at my table."

Scott and Liam exchanged a glance and turned to him as one. Both nodded with enthusiasm.

"Please," Liam said, and Niall could tell he wasn't feigning the gratefulness that seeped through. "Every time I go to dinner, I feel as if I'm prey. Someone is stalking me for dinner." He shuddered.

Scott gave an emphatic nod. "Liam is not exaggerating. Somehow, you must ensure clans don't subject future participants to such immense pressure to arrive home with mates. I have no idea how you'll do it, but I feel sorry for some attendees. Some packs have scraped and saved for their people to attend. That creates expectations."

Niall tapped his finger against his chin. Neither he nor

Angus had anticipated this, and he doubted a solution existed. He'd wanted attendees to enjoy the experience and connect openly with fellow shifters. "I might use the remaining few days to chat with those left."

"See, that's the problem right there. Those left feel like failures. It's difficult not to feel rejected when it's such a joyous time for others," Scott pointed out.

"Scott's right. We've enjoyed ourselves but have lives we want to return to and our passion for farming. Others don't have the same luxury. Perhaps provide a partial refund or complimentary attendance for the next gathering. I mean, if it doesn't cut into the bottom line too much."

"Angus and I will consider everything you've mentioned. We could conduct a questionnaire to gather feedback on how to improve the next gathering," Niall said. "There's time for a survey."

"You should do that," Liam said. "Honestly, it will be good to get home. I'll have the luxury of knowing if anyone is staring at me, it'll be the cows impatient for their morning hay."

Scott laughed, but Niall could see Liam truly was uneasy. Something to remember because attendees weren't meant to feel stressed or pressured. He'd wanted shifters to relax with others and enjoy social interaction.

Simple pleasures were everything. It made him even more determined to claim Suzie to experience this freedom and joy with his mate. Maybe with his children, too.

His bear chuffed at this thought. They were in complete agreement. Suzie belonged with them, and they needed to persuade her of this truth.

At last, the day of their flight arrived. Every part of Niall knew his decision to go to Suzie was right, even if she ignored his messages. He needed to show Suzie he loved her and would grovel at her feet if necessary. He understood now that Suzie was essential to his well-being, and while he'd waited to go to her, he'd written her letters. They were in his carryon, and he hoped she'd read them. He'd also collected some other things for his win-Suzie-over arsenal. He crossed his fingers that they'd help.

Scott joined him, his luggage in tow. "Have you seen Liam?"

"No," Niall said.

"He left the bar early and told me he intended to pack. When I arrived back at our room, most of his stuff was gone. I wasn't worried and fell asleep, but he wasn't there when I woke. Niall, I haven't seen him since last night." Scott's brow crinkled. "Now I come to think of it—there was a strange smell in our room because I opened the window. I thought it was cleaning products."

"Angus!" Niall shouted.

Angus glided into the room. "No reason to holler like a common guttersnipe."

Niall chuffed, chastened. "Sorry. Have you seen Liam? Scott hasn't seen him since last night when he left the bar."

"No, but let me ask my team." He pulled a phone from his pocket and pressed a button. Seconds later, he was firing questions. His expression was grim when he hung up. "My team will search, but no one has seen him. Our security cameras suffered a strange blip just after midnight, but they came back online. Scott, can you find something personal of Liam's? Our team will attempt to track him."

"Sure, a stack of his shirts is still on his bed. I'll grab them for you."

After Scott's departure, Niall faced Angus. "I don't like this. Has anyone else left or disappeared during the same time frame? It could guide us."

Angus nodded. "I had the same thought, and one of my team is already checking." His expression tightened. "Is Scott certain Liam didn't meet someone?"

"Liam mentioned feeling as if someone was watching him. We discussed the gathering and the pressure alphas put on their people to produce results."

"It's all right if a couple are mates, but abduction is unacceptable," Angus stated, his narrow face stony with disapproval.

"I agree."

Scott returned. "This is one of Liam's shirts. It was the one he was wearing before dinner yesterday."

Angus gave a clipped nod and frowned. "What about Liam's passport? Has that gone?"

"No, it was in the room safe," Scott said. "Liam's wallet was there as well. We locked our passports away before running since we didn't want to lose them."

Angus glanced at his wristwatch. "If you don't leave for the airport, you'll miss your plane."

Niall hesitated, knowing Angus was right but torn. Scott's expression suggested he felt the same dilemma. He

SHELLEY MUNRO

wanted to go home, but loyalty to his friend would make him stay.

"You must go," Angus said. "My team and I will search for Liam. We'll have found him by the time you reach New Zealand."

The confidence in Angus seemed to settle Scott's anxiety, while Niall's bear just wanted Suzie.

"I promise I will find Liam and help him deal with whatever mess he's found himself in," Angus promised. "My team is professional and has more experience in security matters and search and rescue than you. Let the experts deal with this."

"What do you think?" Niall asked Scott.

"I want to go home, but Liam is my friend. Let me call Saber and talk to him."

Niall nodded, understanding. "Use my office."

Scott was back in five minutes and held the phone out to Angus. "Saber would like to speak with you."

Angus took the phone without hesitation.

"What did he say?" Niall asked.

"He told me to come home. Saber said if Liam didn't turn up, we'd assemble a team from home and return to search. Saber also reminded me that Liam is a survivor and has a brain. If Liam can, he'll contact us."

Angus ended the call with Saber and glanced expectantly at them. "Are you ready to leave?"

Before Niall could reply, his bear gave a loud chuff.

Scott laughed. "We'll take that as a yes."

23

THICK-HEADED BEAR

S UZIE MISSED NIALL, EVEN though she was still angry with the thick-headed bear and ignoring his messages and texts. They'd separated mere days ago, but it felt like a part of her was empty, and only Niall could fill that space. She growled out a naughty word and thumped her hands on her piano keyboard. The discordant notes echoed in the tiny room, and her breath hissed out. If she continued like this, she'd wake her parents, and they needed their rest.

Her father had been in a rare state when Suzie arrived home and hadn't settled until Gavin had allowed her mother to leave the clinic. Her injuries had taken time to knit together, even with rapid shifter healing. With her father so stressed, Suzie was caring for her siblings. They, of course, were acting out more than usual. Suzie got it. Their parents' accident had scared them and made everyone realize that despite a shifter's toughness, they weren't invincible.

Suzie ran her hands across the keys, focusing on composing her desired song. Another pithy curse emerged, and she squeezed her eyes shut, wishing Edwina was here. She'd wrangle this tune in no time while Suzie focused on the lyrics.

This was a cheerful, upbeat song, but everything that emerged was heartbreak and he-done-me-wrong.

Suzie sighed and pushed away from the piano. She'd be better off clearing the breakfast dishes and deciding what to prepare for dinner—a meaty soup. Gavin had suggested making a beef broth for her mother, which would also work for her father. Also, there were after-school snacks to prepare for her siblings. They were always ravenous after a day of learning and playing with their friends.

Maybe she'd bake some bread. The kneading process might aid her temper that lurked in the background. So far, she'd held everything together, but the longer she thought about Niall, the deeper the anger bubbled in her. That she could miss the man and experience such deep resentment was contradictory. Illogical. But she'd like to knock sense into the stubborn bear. Her family was nothing like his. While her parents were still unwell and off balance, they were a loving family and supportive of one another. Niall didn't understand because his childhood had been horrid.

Some of her anger had dispersed, but boy, it had hurt when he hadn't understood why she needed to leave Scotland earlier than planned.

A car door slam had Suzie jerking from her thoughts

and hurrying to the front door. Their doorbell was loud, and she didn't want their visitor to wake her parents. The piano room was insulated, but not the rest of the house.

Suzie flung open the door and blinked. Scott lifted his hand in farewell while a diffident Niall stood before her, his expression blank apart from his eyes. She could see his bear peeking at her, and her silly heart lurched.

She cleared her throat. "Why are you here?"

"Are you not going to invite me inside?" Niall countered, his familiar husky voice doing things to her insides.

She steeled herself when part of her wanted to throw herself into his arms. "I don't want to wake my parents."

"How is your mother?"

Gah! They sounded like polite acquaintances. "Want to go for a drive? I'll give you a tour of Middlemarch, and we can stop by the cafe for coffee."

Niall smiled then, the corners of his eyes crinkling. *So cute! No!* Devil take it, she was furious with this man. He needed to apologize.

Niall offered his arm. Suzie blinked and shrugged off his gentlemanly aid.

"The car is this way." Suzie stalked in the right direction.

Once she sat behind the wheel, she realized her hands were shaking. What did the man want? Why was he here? Curling her fingers around the wheel, she took a deep breath and started the vehicle. She drove away from the house, exhaling when her confidence returned.

"When did you arrive?" *So polite. Her mother would be proud.*

"Scott and I flew in this morning," Niall said.

She frowned. "What about Liam?"

"Liam is missing, presumed abducted. Angus is searching for clues, but we haven't found one yet."

"What?" Concern filled Suzie, and she wanted to demand why Niall and Scott hadn't remained in Scotland until they found Liam. "You think one of the other shifters spirited Liam away?"

"That's what it looks like. Scott, Liam, and I went for a run the day before Liam disappeared. We know Liam wasn't interested in anyone. His passport and wallet were in the safe, and some of his clothes were still unpacked. It looks as if someone scooped him up and grabbed his bag before fleeing. The cameras didn't pick up anything."

"Liam should be okay, right?"

"We're hoping he won't come to any harm," Niall said. "I feel bad for leaving, but I know Angus is searching for him. Angus feels affronted that someone got past his security. He'll look upon this as a challenge."

"You still haven't said why you're here," Suzie said, keeping her gaze on the road ahead. *Not doing so well in the tourist guide stakes.*

"Wait until you're not driving. Make no mistake, I know exactly why I'm here, but I want your full attention when we talk."

The man had never been super chatty unless it came to honey. That truly was his passion, and his enthusiasm was contagious. "Not going to give me a clue?"

"You didn't respond to my messages or answer my calls."

Suzie released an impatient sigh and made no secret of

her displeasure. "Fine. I've already told you Middlemarch is small and countryside surrounds the town. The land we're driving past now belongs to my family. My grandfather and father. The Mitchells' land flanks ours. The Mitchell twins, that is. Their older brothers Saber and Felix own another large block of land while Leo runs the vineyard." Suzie rattled off the owners of the land they passed, their progress toward town slow because they encountered a farmer shifting his herd of Hereford cattle along the road.

"Bees are much easier to care for than these large beasts. Are those alpacas?"

"Yes, that's Mitchell land. When I was a kid, they had mainly sheep, but they diversified when the market fell. They still have sheep, but they also have cattle, alpacas, and, as I mentioned, a vineyard over Cromwell way."

"Makes sense. A bad honey season was why Angus and I started the gathering. We also rent out the castle to business groups for conferences and to regular tourists during the height of summer."

Once they'd maneuvered past the cattle, old Mr. McWilliams tractor slowed them down. Suzie waved when he pulled over to let them pass.

She pointed out the school, the police station, the vet, a vehicle service station, a dress shop, and a supermarket. "This is the cafe," she said, pulling into a parking space. Her stomach quivered as sudden nerves assailed her.

Suzie was acutely aware of Niall following her up the footpath to the front door. The green scent from the rose bushes seemed especially strong, almost nauseating, on this bright winter day. She breathed through her mouth, and her breath emerged in puffs of steam. Two steps led up to a wooden verandah, hanging baskets full of trailing greenery bright against the stained wood.

The doorbell tingled as she pushed the door open and held it for Niall. Coffee plus the sweet, sugary scent of baking hit her, and more of her angst faded. He was here. A man wouldn't travel halfway across the world to see her without reason. She tried to tell herself that. Tried to listen, but fear darted in, adding to her confusion.

"Would you like coffee?" Niall asked.

Suzie nodded at one of the staff. "A latte, please, plus a cheese scone. I'll grab a table." She pointed at one in the corner and retreated, turning her back on him and her discombobulation. When he'd disagreed with her leaving Scotland, she'd been furious. Disappointed. However, her positive outlook prompted her to view this as a sign to attend university. Calls to Edwina had gone unanswered, but instinct told her Edwina wasn't returning home. She'd met Edwina's mother in the supermarket, but from what she'd said, she had expected her daughter to arrive home with Scott and Liam.

Edwina's grandmother had held an air of smugness and suppressed excitement, but Suzie knew better than to ask questions. Still, it had made her uneasy, and she'd feel better once she spoke with her friend.

Suzie slid into a chair and closed her eyes. It felt like she stood in a mushy swamp and was slowly sinking, no matter how hard she tried to reach solid ground.

"What's wrong?" Niall's low voice came.

She jolted, her eyes flying open. He pulled out the chair next to her instead of the one opposite. Seconds later, his big hands cupped one of hers.

"I'm sorry, Suzie. I didn't understand until you'd left how much you meant to me. You're more important than my honey. Much more important. Waking up in my bed without you by my side felt wrong. I need you."

But did he love her?

What if he felt companionship, and she'd simply become a habit for him? She'd seamlessly slotted into his life, and now he was taking her for granted. Her ideal man should require her as much as she needed him. Like her next breath. And she wanted respect, dammit. Then there was her family. She loved her parents and her brother and sisters. They were a close family. Sure, they had dramas because they were normal shifters. They laughed together and fought together. It was what families did.

She glanced at Niall and found him frowning. He tilted his head, looking as if he was silently debating with himself.

"This is coming out wrong." He tugged on his hair. "Suzie, I l—" He broke off abruptly when Emily, the cafe's owner, arrived with two cups of coffee and two scones.

"Thanks, Emily," Suzie said when it appeared Niall wouldn't do anything other than scowl. A little devil prompted her to push him. "Niall, this is Emily. She's Saber's wife."

Niall nodded. "We met this morning. Scott and I visited Saber. I wanted him to know I was visiting his town and to give him a progress report on the search for Liam."

Suzie blinked, baffled that he'd thought and planned when she'd assumed he'd charged in like a raging bear.

"We did," Emily said and grinned. Before she turned away, Suzie caught the woman waggling her eyebrows. She winked at Suzie.

Suzie frowned.

"Is something wrong?" Niall asked.

"No." She picked up a cup and took a sip. "Ugh! Too sweet. I think this is your coffee." She shunted it toward him.

Niall ignored the coffee, his expression one of frustration. "Suzie," he said, his voice tight with suppressed tension. "I—"

"There's Scott," Suzie said and jumped to her feet.

Niall's bark of aggravation had her flinching, but she wove through the tables to reach Scott.

"Hi," she said. "Niall said Liam is missing."

Scott's brows drew together. "Niall and Saber are in close contact with Angus regarding the search, but they haven't found him yet. No one saw him leave the castle."

"That's weird," she said.

"Suzie, I'm trying to speak with you," Niall said. He reminded her of the testy bear she'd first met.

She whirled to glower at him. "You had a chance to talk when we were in Scotland. And you haven't even apologized yet." Belatedly, she realized she'd shouted in the middle of the cafe. Heat raced to her cheeks, and her fists clenched at her sides. The chatter ceased, and everyone stared wide-eyed at her and Niall.

"Why don't you take your coffee and sit outside?" Scott

suggested in a low voice. "It might be cold, but at least you'll have privacy."

Suzie growled. She didn't even attempt to restrain her feline.

"Suzie," Scott snapped, grasping her forearm and dragging her toward the door that led to the outside seating.

Niall strode to their table and grabbed their coffees.

"I'll bring your food," Emily said in a low voice.

Suzie struggled with her temper. She rarely lost it, but she was a volcano when she did. She wrenched her arm from Scott's grip and stomped outdoors. Not even the whoosh of cold air dented her anger. How dare he? She didn't stop when she reached the nearest table, and her restless urge for movement prevented her from sitting. She kicked at a pile of leaves. It wasn't enough.

She whirled and found the bear watching her. And it *was* the bear flashing in Niall's eyes. "What do you want?"

"You," he said, holding her gaze. "I want you."

"Why?" she spat, giving a harsh sigh. "Why do you want me?" Heck, he'd never voiced the L word, and right now, he hadn't mentioned they were mates. She had no idea what he expected from her.

Finally, finally, emotion slid across his face, and what she saw had her holding her breath.

Niall crossed the distance between them and reached for her hands. The warmth from his palms was almost searing, and it shook her. "Suzie, I love you. You're my mate, and I can't live a diminished life without you. I'm so sorry for how I treated you when you needed my support." He paused to pull a packet of what looked like letters from his pocket and handed them to her. "When you didn't answer my messages, I wrote you a letter. It turned into a long letter. There's some other stuff there, too."

She stared at him wordlessly, blinking slowly as she noticed the number of envelopes. Her mind didn't help her formulate a reply, so she kept staring at him.

"Say something," he said, his expression uncertain. "Please."

That vulnerability jolted her brain into gear. "You love me?"

"Since we first made love, my bear and I fell. That first day when I thought you were my temporary secretary, I saw you. My bear saw you. But we're males. Sometimes, we have thick heads and are slow to make decisions. We behave stupidly. I love you, and I'm sorry I behaved like an idiot when you told me you had to come home. Once you'd left, I realized how much of a jerk I'd been. Please marry me, Suzie. I want to spend my life making you happy and helping you to achieve your dreams."

Finally, she found her voice, but her heart pitter-pattered so hard she could barely hear herself think. "You truly love me?"

"Yes, sweetheart. I can't imagine my life without you. My business is in Scotland, but you can visit your loved ones as often as you want. They are always welcome to stay with us." He grinned. "I have friends in Middlemarch, too. So, will you marry me?"

24

MEET MUM AND DAD

N IALL'S HEART BEAT LIKE a drum while he waited for her reply. He thought she'd say yes, but his bear's agitation had him wanting to pace. She wouldn't say no, would she? She couldn't. No, it didn't matter. He'd prove to her he was worth the risk, no matter how long it took.

Niall took a deep breath and fought for calm. "Please, take a seat."

Suzie dropped onto one of the bench seats. "You love me?"

"Yes, very much. I want a future with you. I'm sorry for my behavior. Truly, I messed up, and I wish I could take everything I said back and start over." He scanned her face, terrified to decipher her expression. He was on the verge of speaking, pleading for her to consider a life together, when she smiled softly. That smile grew until it was as broad and bright as the sun.

"Oh, Niall. Why didn't you voice your thoughts then? Tell me you loved me? I would've come back."

Niall grunted, uncomfortable with the truth. He had to explain why he'd said the wrong thing and caused her to leave under such a black cloud. "I panicked," he said, finding the tightness of his chest easing now that he was telling the truth. "In that moment, it resembled rejection, bringing back a flood of family memories. I was a broken man when I arrived in Scotland. It took me a long time to trust the laird and Angus."

Suzie patted his arm. "Don't you see? Angus and the laird became your family. You had a family that mistreated you, but when you left, you found another family who loved and supported you. A found family, and you'll have an even bigger one after we marry."

Hope rose in him. "After we're married?"

"Yes, Niall. I love you. Don't you know me well enough to understand that I wouldn't have slept with you if I didn't care for you? You're my mate. When we're together, I feel whole and like to think you feel the same way."

"I didn't come to New Zealand intending to leave again without you," he murmured.

When he glanced at her this time, the deep emotion he saw shook him. Her features were softer, and her beautiful green eyes glowed with happiness, with contentment, with love. Niall slid along the bench seat and took her hand in his. "I brought a ring with me. It belonged to the laird's mother, and he gave it to me to give to the woman I fell in love with." His mind drifted to the elderly man. Suzie was right. He'd become Niall's family, and Angus was still his family. He loved and respected the elderly shifter. "If you don't like it, we can have it redesigned, or I could buy you another."

Suzie grinned. "Show me."

He retrieved a ring box from his pocket and opened it to reveal the antique golden ring featuring diamonds and rubies. The ring had held significant meaning for the laird, symbolizing the elderly Scotsman's love for his wife and for Niall. He'd absorbed more than he'd thought but never considered himself part of a family. Until today.

A sense of gratefulness assailed him as he replayed Suzie's fervent words. He had a family who loved him. They might not be blood relations, but that didn't matter. They loved and respected him, and he knew without asking that he could call on them, and they'd come. He briefly thought of the two brothers who'd traveled to Scotland with mischief in mind and substantial gambling debts. They'd seen him as an easy way out of their problems.

Niall shifted his attention to Suzie, who remained fixated on the ring. "Do you like it?"

"Yes." She glanced at him, her eyes green pools of awe and amazement. "So much. I'd be honored to wear it."

Thankful again, Niall tugged the ring free and slid it onto Suzie's finger. They studied it for a beat longer before their gazes connected.

"Suzie, I love you. Marry me soon?"

Instead of agreeing, she said, "How long can you stay? Could you do two weeks?"

Alarm slammed through him. A trace of panic. Was she changing her mind already?

"Niall?"

Her utter calmness allowed him to breathe. She said yes, he reminded himself, but it told him how off-balance he was with love and family. He'd programmed himself to fear the worst. He had to improve because Suzie needed the best version of him. She deserved nothing less.

"After you left and we discovered Michael was behind everything, the honey didn't seem important. Angus and I discussed it and we've put back the release date. With all the upheaval, we decided it would be best to wait. Besides, I couldn't focus. The excitement had gone because you weren't there to share it with me. I missed you. You're more critical to me than the honey."

Suzie laughed then and squeezed his hand. "I have a suggestion. Why don't we plan to get married before we return to Scotland? Set the date in two weeks. Angus might not make it, but we could have another ceremony in Scotland. What do you think?"

Niall didn't hesitate. "I'd like that very much. We'll have a party when we get home, but we could also set up a link for Angus to watch the ceremony."

"Is it safe to come out?" Scott called.

"No," Suzie said. "He hasn't kissed me yet."

Niall rose with alacrity and scooped her off the bench. He hauled her into his arms and breathed in her scent. He playfully smooched the tip of her nose before grinning at her. "Would you like a kiss to celebrate our engagement?"

"Yes, please." Her prim tone contrasted with her

mirthful eyes.

"Your wish is my command," he said.

She was still rolling her eyes when he claimed her mouth, and he settled in to kiss the stuffing out of her. Passion flared between them. A sense of rightness and happiness filled Niall as Suzie's arms surrounded him.

"Everything seems peaceful," Scott said in a loud voice.

Suzie laughed against Niall's lips, and he lifted his head to grin at their friend. "She said yes. We're getting married in two weeks before we return to Scotland."

Scott let out a whoop, and Niall's grin widened.

"Congratulations!" a feminine voice said.

"Thanks, Emily," Suzie said.

"Will your parents be well enough to attend your wedding?" Niall asked.

"I think so," Suzie said. "Hopefully, it will give them something to look forward to."

"Would you like the reception here?" Emily asked. "Catering will be easy since everyone will want to help."

"That would be awesome," Suzie said, squeezing Niall's hand again. "Gran's garden is beautiful. Thoughts on a garden wedding and our reception here?"

"And another in the castle chapel," Niall said, his bear giving an enthusiastic chuff that echoed through his mind.

Suzie's smile was once again full of sunshine, happiness, and contentment. "I'd like that. Maybe I'll finally contact Edwina, and she can come. I'd like you to meet my best friend."

"Anything for you," Niall whispered.

Scott groaned. "Okay, now you're just getting soppy.

Enough of that."

"*Ooh*, you have a ring," Emily said, her brown eyes full of nosy interest and enthusiasm. "Let me see."

Niall watched with pride as the two women discussed the ring. His laird would approve of Suzie, and he knew Suzie had Angus's blessing. Niall would've claimed her anyway because she made him happy, but Angus's high regard meant a lot. He only hoped Suzie's family thought he was good enough for their daughter and sister.

An hour later, he and Suzie were in the kitchen with Suzie's siblings, the large box of tablet he'd brought from Scotland open on the table.

"Do you really change into a bear?" Suzie's brother asked, his green eyes full of the same curiosity Niall often saw in Suzie. Her brother plucked a piece of tablet from the box and stuffed it inside his mouth.

"Yes." Niall winked at Suzie.

A laugh trembled her shoulders, but she held in her amusement.

"Can you show us?" Suzie's youngest sister asked, showing similar interest.

Niall tilted his head. "What happens if you try to shift while still wearing your clothes?"

"Our shirts and trousers rip, and Mum shouts at us because clothing is expensive, you know," Suzie's other sister said.

"Yeah," her brother said. "I had to mow the lawn for a whole month when I did it last time. I forgot," he added ruefully.

Niall nodded. "Well, I don't want to destroy my clothes.

Also, I think your parents are coming downstairs, and the last thing I want is for them to see my naked backside."

"Even though your bottom is very sexy, I think it's best if you remain clothed in these circumstances," Suzie murmured under the cover of loud laughter.

Niall winked at her, his heart swelling with such love and joy that he never wanted to leave this room. But footsteps from behind had him rising, respect something the laird had drummed into him. A woman—an older version of Suzie limped down the stairs. A tall, slim man with a pale face covered with cuts and bruises followed her. His gait held a slight hitch, and Niall wanted to go to their aid. He didn't, seeing stiff pride in the older couple. The injuries must've been severe for them to still bear cuts and bruises.

"Come and sit by me," Suzie said, tugging at his elbow.

He acquiesced, leaving the chair at the head of the table for Suzie's father.

Suzie's mother appeared as tired as her husband, and it was clear to Niall that Suzie's parents had needed her. He'd been the idiot. Suzie reached for his hand, and he linked their fingers beneath the table.

"Mum, Dad, this is Niall," Suzie said, her calm voice holding none of the nerves he felt in the tremor of her hand. She cleared her throat. "Niall asked me to marry him."

Suzie's mother gasped, while Niall found himself under the intense scrutiny of Suzie's father.

"You never mentioned a man," Suzie's mother said.

Niall felt Suzie stiffen, but he held his tongue. He was the stranger here, although that would change.

243

"I met Niall at the gathering," Suzie said. "Niall is my mate. Would you care for a cup of tea?"

Her words fell into silence, and Niall watched Suzie's parents exchange a glance. He nodded at Suzie, and she rose to make another pot of tea.

Silence fell again.

"I'm pleased to meet you," Niall said. "Suzie mentions her family often, so I was looking forward to making your acquaintance."

"You're not from here," Suzie's mother said.

"I live in Scotland."

Suzie's mother and father exchanged another meaningful glance.

"We'd hoped Suzie would remain at home to help while we're recovering," Suzie's father said.

A knock sounded on the door, and Niall's breath eased out, glad of the interruption. This wasn't going well, and judging from Suzie's expression, she hadn't expected this reaction. Her mother was still unwell—true, but she was healing.

"I'll get the door," Suzie's brother said when the knock came again.

"Mum, Dad. I don't understand," Suzie said, her voice controlled. "My university course starts soon. That was always the plan."

"We need you here," her father said, speaking for the first time.

"It's Saber," Suzie's brother said.

Niall nodded at the feline shifter as Saber paused in the doorway.

"Moira. Donald. Moira, you're looking much better than when I last saw you," Saber said. "I wanted to check on you and ask a favor. One of Rory's younger wolves asked if anyone was hiring. He wants to work with animals rather than in the woodworking business. He has helped Felix and me when we need an extra pair of hands. I wondered if you could give him a job."

Suzie frowned, and Niall's stomach dipped. Was money an issue? He could hire a farmhand but didn't want to damage the man's pride.

"Suzie will work on the farm," her father announced.

Niall mentally reshuffled their plans. He might need to return to Scotland, but he could also work remotely. He opened his voice to speak, then pressed his lips together. Despite his desire to assist, he couldn't fix this problem. If he interfered, Suzie might resent it. Staying silent was the hardest thing he'd done.

"Dad, no. Niall is my mate, and I need to spend time with him. Once we're married, we'll return to Scotland. While we're here, Niall and I will help as much as possible, and I'll train the new worker."

Her father sighed, and a faint flush covered his cheeks. "We can't afford a farm hand."

"Dad, of course you can. Since I'm not attending university, I'll return the money you gave me. It's sufficient for wages."

"You're not going to university?" her mother asked. "You've been saving for years. What will Edwina say? You were going together."

"Edwina found a mate too, or at least he found her.

I'm hoping she'll contact me soon. As for my music, I'm not giving up. Niall found me a course that I can take in Edinburgh. It's not that far from where we'll live. Once Edwina contacts me, we should manage to collaborate. I'm not abandoning anything. I'm gaining a mate and a beautiful home in Scotland. You'll see when you and Dad visit," Suzie said.

"Is that true? You'll allow Suzie to continue with her studies?" her mother demanded of Niall.

"Yes, of course. Your daughter is a force of nature. You must realize I don't have a choice if I want her to stay with me," Niall said. "I want her to follow her dream, so I researched courses she might like and brought the information with me. It appears she has settled on one in Edinburgh."

"You love her," her father said.

Niall met his gaze without flinching. "More than anything. Suzie is my other half."

"What do you do in Scotland?" her father asked.

Suzie spoke quietly with Saber. Saber nodded and left.

"I produce honey," Niall said.

"You're a bear," Suzie's father said.

"Ah, you heard the bit about shifting and bare bottoms," Niall said.

"We did."

"I have a natural aptitude for honey, so it made sense to embrace my strengths. I have a talent for finding honey blends that resonate with the public. Do you have honey producers here? It's too cold right now but during the summer?"

Donald frowned. "Could we do that to generate more income?"

"I can research it for you," Niall said. "If honey production is viable during the warmer months, we could put in several hives. I'd be happy to invest."

Donald nodded, accepting a mug of tea from Suzie. "Thank you. I've been trying to think of ways to diversify. I'd appreciate your help."

The residual tension leached from the room, and Niall relaxed.

"Have you set a date for your wedding?" her mother asked.

"Two weeks." Suzie grinned. "We're getting married in grandmother's garden and having the reception at the cafe or the hall. It depends on how many people we invite." She glanced at Niall. "We'd prefer something intimate."

Suzie's parents exchanged another glance, this time with a smile that eased Niall's mind. They weren't objecting to him marrying their daughter.

"Two weeks it is," Donald said.

"Suzie, you'll find a notepad in the drawer beside you. We'd better make lists."

Suzie followed her mother's instructions, winking at Niall as she did so. Everything would work out fine.

25

HAPPY, HAPPY

T HE DAY DAWNED CRISP with the promise of sun despite her grandmother fretting about a winter wedding. Suzie didn't care about the weather. All she wanted was to marry Niall, and that would happen today, one way or another, since she and Niall had formulated a Plan B. Many chaperones had limited their time together, so it was just as well they'd decided not to formalize their mating until they married.

Earlier, she had reread Niall's letters, which brought tears to her eyes. He had expressed regret for his behavior and promised to do much better in using his words and trying to understand her point of view. An excellent reminder that communication was important. He'd also mentioned his research of music courses, and since his arrival, they'd discussed this and her preference for the course at Edinburgh University. With Niall sitting beside her, she'd enrolled yesterday. So exciting! They'd talked a lot since becoming engaged, and although they'd probably argue again in the future, Suzie felt they were better equipped to come out the other side.

Soon, they'd become husband and wife.

And she couldn't wait to get Niall to herself.

Alone.

Suzie hummed under her breath, still thrilled at a romantic song she and Edwina had composed last year. It was perfect for her to walk down the aisle toward Niall and the wedding celebrant.

Her father tapped on her bedroom door. "Are you ready?"

Suzie grinned, pure happiness fizzing through her and finding an outlet in that smile. "Ready!"

She wore a sleek cream dress with a matching shawl because, although it was sunny, it was still wintery. Her mother had helped her apply subtle makeup and style a casual updo. Suzie felt pretty, and yes, she was ready to embrace the future with Niall.

"You look beautiful, sweetheart," her father said. Only one still-healing cut remained on his cheek. Her mother walked with a slight limp, but her rapid progress had pleased Gavin.

"Thanks. Mum helped."

"We like your young man," her mother said on entering the bedroom.

"Me, too," Suzie said, her voice bubbling with laughter. "I think I might marry him."

"Are you certain?" her father asked, his tone serious.

"We can run."

Suzie chortled, catching the lurking humor in her father's eyes. "He's my mate, Dad. I love him."

"Well then," her mother said with an emphatic nod. "We'd better hustle. We have a wedding to attend."

Suzie was still grinning when she followed her parents outside into the sunshine. Her mother handed her a bouquet of yellow daisies, then she took her father's arm.

"Thank you," she said. "This is beautiful. Amazing." Her grandmother and mother had worked miracles in the garden, and once a guitar started playing their song, her father led her up a makeshift aisle outlined with pots of yellow daisies. Family and locals sat on both sides on garden benches. Some elders had lap rugs. Ahead, in front of a flower arbor, Niall stood with Scott and the male celebrant. She frowned briefly since they still hadn't heard from Liam. Suzie hoped he was safe.

Her attention went to Niall, and their gazes connected. She couldn't wait for the coming evening. Her smile started slowly, but Niall caught it and echoed the curve of lips. Stars, she loved the big man. Her mate. She shuddered inwardly because the anticipation of the coming intimacy and the idea of marking Niall as her forever mate was heady stuff.

The slow march up the aisle took ages. Soft exclamations reached her—compliments for her dress and her hair. Relief at her parents' state of health.

"I imagined this moment," her father whispered. "But I didn't realize how proud I'd feel and how excited I am to watch you embrace the next stage of your life. We'll miss you when you travel to Scotland."

Suzie choked up but managed a few words. "You can visit."

"We can't afford it, sweetheart."

Suzie glanced at Niall. "You know the castle where they hold the gathering?"

"Yes."

"Niall hates to boast, but he owns part of that, and his honey business does well. Niall has money, Dad. Lots of it, and he wants me to be happy. We'll visit as often as possible but can pay for your flights to Scotland. You're Niall's family now, and better, he likes and respects you. Let him help you."

Her father blinked as they reached Niall before kissing her cheek and placing her hand in Niall's.

"Dad?"

"I'll think about it. A castle," he muttered as he joined her mother. "Wow."

Suzie grinned at Niall and handed her bouquet to her younger sister. "Hi, handsome. Want to get married?"

"I thought you'd never ask," Niall said. He kissed her cheek and turned them to face the smiling wedding celebrant. The wedding celebrant's brown eyes twinkled beneath bushy eyebrows.

"Shall we get this party started? Dear friends and family. I welcome you here to witness the exchange of vows between Suzie and Niall."

Suzie's childhood wedding daydreams had been grander than this low-key reality, but the simplicity didn't matter. Her nearest and dearest were here, and she was marrying the man she loved. Her only regret was Edwina's absence, but she'd finally spoken to her friend. They'd made plans to catch up online once Suzie returned to Scotland.

The ceremony went amazingly fast, and her heart sang with joy.

"You may now kiss your bride," the wedding celebrant said.

Niall turned to her, his happiness blazing in his features as his gaze dropped to her lips. It was time for their first kiss as a married couple. And what a kiss. It started slowly and gradually ramped up until her knees weakened, and she had to clutch Niall's shoulders. When they finally parted, everyone clapped and cheered.

"I love you, Mr. Sinclair."

"You make me so happy, Mrs. Sinclair," Niall returned. "You are the light of my life. Shall we celebrate?"

She grinned. "Yes."

The wedding breakfast at the cafe was full of happiness, good food, and friendship. The party went late into the night until it was time for them to depart.

"Wait," her youngest sister cried. "You need to throw your bouquet. It's tradition."

Suzie shared a laughing glance with Niall. "All right. You organize everyone, and I'll prepare to throw."

Her sister snapped orders at her friends, and they ran off to gather the Middlemarch singles.

"I can't wait to get you on your own," Niall murmured.

"Same page," Suzie said. "It feels as if the last time we were alone was weeks ago."

"It was," Niall growled.

"Everyone is ready outside," her sister said, beaming with satisfaction. "We collected all the singles." She leaned closer. "Wolves, felines, and a few humans." She rubbed her tiny hands together, patches of excitement glowing on her cheeks. "I can't wait to see who gets your bouquet. Come on!"

Bemused, Suzie followed her sister outside, and Niall trailed them. Suzie blinked at the crowd. She'd assumed her sister and her friends would collect the unmarried women, but no. Confused males shuffled their feet amongst dozens of single women. Her sister and young friends ringed the entire group, resembling sentries holding a crowd at bay.

"Ready?" Suzie asked, and everyone fell silent.

"To catch the bouquet?" Henry, a single wolf, asked disgustedly. "Really? I'm out!"

Suzie grinned and turned without another word. As the bouquet left her hands, several voices cried out in dismay.

"No!" came an irate male voice.

Suzie stifled a giggle, satisfied with her true aim, while Henry glared at the daisy bouquet in his hands and shook his head. He glanced in Suzie and Niall's direction, and when he found them grinning at him, he glowered. He thrust the bouquet at the nearest woman. "You take it," he snapped and stomped away.

"You can run but can't hide," Niall murmured.

"Yeah," Suzie said. "I believe in the bouquet's power. I caught one at my cousin's wedding six months ago."

"We're fated mates," Niall said with satisfaction.

"I can't wait to get to the good stuff and claim you."

"Me, too," Niall agreed while they gave their thanks and made their goodbyes.

Their farewells were lengthy, and she thought Niall might've been impatient. Relief filled her on checking his expression, along with a touch of awe. Niall radiated happiness. Her friends and family had taken to him immediately, and he was blooming under the acceptance. Her friends were the best. Scott had introduced Niall to those he hadn't met during the days before their wedding, and he and Scott had gone for a run with the Mitchell brothers. He'd toured their vineyard and mixed with tigers, leopards, and wolves without missing a blink.

Niall opened the door of his rental car for her and closed it again once she'd settled in the passenger seat. He hurried around to the driver's side and climbed inside. Before he started the vehicle, he said, "I've had a lovely day. Everyone has made me so welcome because I was smart enough to fall in love with you. But I must admit. I'm pleased we're alone now."

"Me too," Suzie said.

Niall drove the quick trip to the country resort where he'd been staying. Suzie had popped by to pick up Niall several times but hadn't set foot inside. Butterflies danced around her belly, but they were the good kind.

Niall jumped from the vehicle and was around it before she moved. He opened the door. "I'm going to miss your friends and your family, even your siblings," he said with a grin. "Saber asked if he could bring Emily to visit. He's planning a surprise trip for her."

"My grandmother told me you taught her how to make

an online call. She is eager to try her skills once we return home." Home. That was precisely how Scotland felt, and that told her everything. Niall *was* home.

They entered the luxurious cabin together. Niall had told her that although secluded, the lodge had every amenity.

Suzie admired the open-plan room. The place oozed elegant class and comfort.

"Want a drink or anything to eat?" Niall asked.

"No, thanks," Suzie said.

"Thank goodness!" Niall plucked her off her feet, and she shrieked with joy.

"I could've walked," she protested.

"Yes, but I like you in my arms."

He set her on her feet in the bedroom. A massive bed occupied the room, and a slightly open door indicated an attached bathroom on the right.

"I have to keep pinching myself." Niall traced a finger down her cheek, his expression full of tenderness.

Suzie laughed and brushed his hair off his face. "Our marriage does seem dreamlike."

He froze at her touch, hesitating before he kissed her.

"Is something wrong?" Suzie asked, pulling back a fraction when he lifted his mouth.

"It's difficult to control myself when my bear is urging me to hustle. He wants the claiming done so he can bask in having a mate," Niall said dryly. "It's weird because I want the same thing, but I'd hate to scare you."

"Niall." Suzie wrapped her hands around his biceps and smiled. "You'd never hurt me—not physically. I'm sure we'll have an argument or two in the future, but we'll settle our differences like adults. I trust you." She wrinkled her nose. "Besides, my control is a little iffy, too. Maybe we shouldn't have waited."

"We did the right thing. I wanted you to be certain, and I figured you'd never go through with the marriage if you didn't love me. Now that we're married, we're stuck together."

"And I couldn't be happier. Take off your suit jacket and tie. I don't want to tear your beautiful clothes." Her hands trembled as she stepped back.

"Let me get the zipper on your gown. Did I tell you how beautiful you look? My mate. When did I ever get so lucky?"

"You say all the right things," Suzie murmured, hiding her smile. In the looks department, she was ordinary. She tiptoed into striking if she smiled, but Niall studied her as if she were a priceless jewel. And that, her grandmother had told her in a satisfied tone, was worth everything. She had caught herself a good one.

Suzie had already known that without her grandmother's approval.

Niall's fingers were cool against her spine as he tugged down her zipper. She suppressed her shiver of awareness as she turned to him. Their gazes met, and her breathing stalled.

"I love you so much," she whispered.

"Show me," he whispered back. His suit jacket and tie flew in different directions, and Suzie chuckled. She let her gown slither to the floor but picked it up and hung her dress before closing the wardrobe door. Her husband stood before her in all his naked glory.

"Nice," she said with honest appreciation. "Someone looks ready for action."

"Your lingerie is beautiful. More thought than substance."

Suzie laughed again. "A present from my grandparents, if you can believe it."

She went to unhook her bra, but Niall halted her.

"Let me," he said, his voice hoarse. "Please."

Suzie blinked at his awe and the open love in his expression. His hands trembled when he placed them on her shoulders, and an answering ripple ran through her stomach.

"I can't believe I'm so nervous," she whispered, meeting his gaze. "I mean, we've done this before."

"This time, it's with commitment and intent. That makes it more significant."

"When did you get so wise?" she teased.

"Angus tells me I'm old before my time."

"He wouldn't say that if he'd seen you this week. You're not old, Niall. You're mature and thoughtful." She grinned on noticing the hint of red on his cheeks.

"Enough talk." With a flick of his fingers, her bra released. He whisked down her panties before taking her hand and leading her to the bed. Instead of scooping her off her feet and settling her on the mattress, he flopped on the bed and held his arms out. She settled on top of him, curling close because it was chilly and he was warm. Their lips met, explored, and Suzie drifted in a world of touch and passion.

Instead of hurrying, he kissed the tip of her nose playfully. Niall nuzzled her neck, and her breath caught, but he moved on, laying a path of kisses along her jawline. She gripped his shoulders tightly, her breath coming in fast pants. This man. He turned her world upside down.

Finally, Niall claimed her lips again, his fingers running down her back to cup her backside. He squeezed her buttocks, making her laugh.

"Not my best feature, buddy."

He lifted his head to wink. "I like all of you. Not one part of you is inferior. Please remember that."

Her man meant it. Every single word. If she weren't already crazy about him, she would've fallen hopelessly then. "I love you, Niall. Kiss me. Mark me. Make me yours."

"Only if you'll return the favor," he said, his tone solemn.

"Always," she said, meaning it with every part of her.

Their loving took on a more serious tone then, their kisses slower and communicating everything. Tenderness. Caring. Love.

Suzie kissed Niall's shoulders, nibbled his neck, and sucked tiny love bites on his chest. She savored each groan that escaped him, each caught breath as he allowed her to explore.

"No more," he gasped and settled in to kiss her again with serious intent. "Mine," he said when their lips parted, and they were both panting.

His hands glided over her body, transmitting silent

messages, and she melted against him, enjoying his solid strength. He shaped her breasts with his big hands, the sweetness of his kiss drawing a ragged gasp from her. The man knew how to kiss. Kisses charged with such warmth. When his lips moved lower, sliding down her neck and skimming across the upper swell of her breasts, she sighed. The wet pull of his mouth on her nipple had her wriggling, silently begging for more.

Niall rolled their bodies to shift position, one hand sliding down her torso to cup her hip.

"Niall," she whispered.

"Am I doing something wrong?" A trace of mischief colored his tone. The man understood precisely what he was doing to her. She ached for him, needing him more than her next breath.

"Please." It was a touch short of begging, and they both knew it.

Niall didn't dally any longer. Smart man. He used his knee to part her thighs and resettled his body. But when she glanced at his face, she saw the same desperation.

"My bear is mighty impatient. I'm fighting a losing battle," he confessed. "He has wanted to claim you from the start."

"My feline wants the same." She winked. "She just has better manners than your bear."

Niall groaned and nibbled the side of her throat, a hairsbreadth from the juncture of her neck and shoulder. He licked the sensitive spot, and a shudder worked through her. That felt amazing. Suzie slid against him, feeling his hardness as she stretched to lick him in the same place. His tremble was gratifying, and she lifted her head to offer him a lazy smile.

"Let's do it together. I dare you to get the timing right and bite me during my orgasm."

"No pressure." His laughing groan had her giggling.

"I'm sure we'll have fun trying," she said primly.

He groaned again, but his fingers tightened against her hips, and he moved a fraction before he guided himself to her entrance. Eagerly, she arched into his stroke and sighed at the sense of fullness as he pushed inside her.

"That feels amazing," she whispered against his neck with an added flicker of her tongue.

"Yes," he said, laving that fleshy spot on her neck.

It was like poking her finger into a light socket, or at least how she imagined this might feel. Everything inside her lit with amplified pleasure. Maybe it was the moment or their intent. Her lungs labored for air, and she gasped, shuddering. Magical.

Niall flexed his hips, invading and retreating. Filling her while he licked and kissed the marking site. Suzie was more hesitant, uncertain because there would be pain but positive she wanted to take this step. This connection between them would only deepen.

Niall gently raked his teeth over her tender skin, and she jumped, her heart beating impossibly fast. The sensations continued to grow until they became overwhelming. He surrounded her with familiar warmth and bulk, and the flash of anxiety faded. She nibbled and sucked, and it was easy to tell he was feeling a similar exhilaration. The slow climb to pleasure was overwhelming but oh-so-good.

Magic suffused her, and her world stopped before instinct drove her to sink her teeth into Niall's neck. As the coppery taste filled her mouth, a slice of pain had her freezing. For an instant, there was stillness and nothing but the tick of a clock. Then Niall's tongue smoothed across his bite mark. Instinct had Suzie mirroring the action, and the pain receded, replaced by pleasure so intense she wasn't confident her body could contain the blissful sensations.

Niall jerked in her arms, his hips surging against hers. She clutched his shoulders, holding tight through this emotional storm that swirled through her, unprepared when she thought she'd known everything.

Suzie gave one final swipe of her tongue and lifted her head. She'd left a red, raised mark on Niall's neck, and curious, she skimmed it with her fingertips.

His soft curse had her jerking away, her heart beating extra fast.

"Sweetheart, you're welcome to touch any time. It's just that was intense. I'll show you what I mean."

Before she could reply, he dragged his tongue over the scar he'd left. It no longer hurt, but the slow sweep of his tongue ignited every nerve ending in her body. Her hips arced upward, making her realize he still impaled her, and they seemed attached more thoroughly than usual. As the thought entered her head, a spasm tore through her. Gods, Niall was right. It was too much. Not enough.

Weakly, she gripped his shoulders and pushed, her breaths harsh in the moonlit bedroom. Niall lifted his head instantly and grinned. She was aware of him and her feline, along with a new presence who gave a loud, pleased chuff.

She giggled at the effervescence that danced through her mind. Niall's bear was delirious with happiness.

"I feel the deeper connection between us," he said with a trace of awe.

"Your bear is a hoot."

"You feel him?"

"He wants to play." The corners of her mouth turned upward into a wide grin. "He's happy."

"We're not going anywhere," Niall said, shifting his hips subtly. Something tugged deep inside her, subsiding when he stilled. "We're still attached."

"I wonder if that's normal." Suzie reached up to kiss him, seemingly not too worried, and another of those spasms rolled through her, full of pleasure. She sighed and cuddled closer, contentment like a cuddly blanket draped around her. Her lips grazed the mark she'd placed on Niall, and he shuddered, his quick jerk leading to a rapid series of clenches in her lower body.

"Will it be like this every time?" Suzie wondered. "Making love with you has always been fun, but this is on another level. I'm tired, but my body is ultra-aware and sensitive. In a good way."

Niall grinned. "It might be a long night."

"At least we'll have time to talk," Suzie said.

"That sounds serious." He paused, hesitating.

"What?"

"Are you truly all right about living in Scotland? I promised the laird I'd make Scotland my home and become a land guardian, but you lack the same connection."

Suzie cupped his face and caught his gaze before she replied. "My sole aspiration was to attend university and reside in Wellington with Edwina. We wanted to branch out and enjoy our independence. We had so much against us. First, neither of our families are wealthy, and we had to earn money to cover what our scholarships didn't. Edwina's grandmother hated the idea of us leaving and was very vocal. My grandmother is her best friend, so they tried to dissuade us." She wrinkled her nose. "I'm unsure where their imaginations went, but it wasn't a good place. In my roundabout way, I'm trying to say my life is with you. Now that I've heard from Edwina, I know she's close when I'm in Scotland."

"You can visit her easily."

"Yes. I'm not saying I won't miss Middlemarch and my family, but I want to be with you. You're my mate and the person I dream of spending my life with. You, Niall." She pressed her fingertips to his lips, and he kissed them, sending a shudder of longing through her. "Are we still attached?"

Niall shifted a fraction, and she felt a faint tug of her flesh deep inside, not unpleasant but different. He immediately resettled so his weight didn't crush her. "We could always experiment a little with our marks," he suggested.

"Is yours sore?"

"No. It's more sensitive and tender than painful."

"Same," Suzie said and grinned. "I'm game. As long as you can control your bear."

Niall huffed, and his bear echoed the sound. Suzie

laughed, so happy she wanted to shout to the rooftops. It gave her a better insight into her parents and their closeness because she suspected that was what it'd be like for her and Niall.

"I know I've said this a lot today, but I truly love you. I'm so happy that my curiosity put me in the right place at the right time."

"Fate," he said in a soft voice, then his mouth was on her mark, and the passion ramped up between them.

Suzie relaxed in her mate's arms, kissing him in return. She belonged here and couldn't wait to see how their lives unfolded. She anticipated they'd make mistakes along the way, but she saw loving and togetherness and a family and friends. It was how one should live life, and she was eager to start the journey with her fantastic mate.

"I love you, Niall." And Suzie settled in to make sure he fully understood this fact.

What has happened to Liam? Why has he disappeared? Did someone kidnap him? I'll bet he's on one rollercoaster of an adventure!

In the meantime, read the bonus short story about Suzie and Edwina's reunion (https://dl.bookfunnel.com/xge6eodljk).

And if you haven't already, why don't you travel into the future and check out the Middlemarch Capture series, where In virus In drives In the In Mitchell In family to find a new home. The first book in the series is **Snared by Saber**, where you'll meet the descendants of the original Mitchell family. (https://shelleymunro.com/books/snared-by-saber/)

Happy reading
Shelley

ABOUT SHELLEY

USA Today bestselling author Shelley Munro lives in Auckland, the City of Sails, with her husband and a cheeky Jack Russell/mystery breed dog.

Typical New Zealanders, Shelley and her husband left home for their big OE soon after they married (translation of New Zealand speak - big overseas experience). A twelve-month-long adventure lengthened to six years of roaming the world. Enduring memories include being almost sat on by a mountain gorilla in Rwanda, lazing on white sandy beaches in India, whale watching in Alaska, searching for leprechauns in Ireland, and dealing with ghosts in an English pub.

While travel is still a big attraction, these days Shelley is most likely found in front of her computer following another love - that of writing stories of contemporary and paranormal romance and adventure. Other interests include watching rugby (strictly for research purposes), cycling, playing croquet and the ukelele, and curling up with an enjoyable book.

Visit Shelley at her Website
https://shelleymunro.com

Join Shelley's Newsletter
https://shelleymunro.com/newsletter

ALSO BY SHELLEY

Paranormal

Middlemarch Shifters
My Scarlet Woman
My Younger Lover
My Peeping Tom
My Assassin
My Estranged Lover
My Feline Protector
My Determined Suitor
My Cat Burglar
My Stray Cat
My Second Chance
My Plan B
My Cat Nap
My Romantic Tangle
My Blue Lady

My Twin Trouble
My Precious Gift
My Grumpy Wolf

Middlemarch Gathering
My Highland Mate
My Highland Fling
My Elusive Mate
My Valiant Princess
My Highland Wedding
My Highland Billionaire

Dragon Investigators
Blue Moon Dragon
Blood Moon Dragon
Black Moon Dragon
Snow Moon Dragon

Dragon Isles
Liza
Cherry
Rena
Sasha